DEATH ON DIAMOND HEAD

A KIMO RIGG MYSTERY

*To the men and women of the
Honolulu Police Department and especially
Deputy Chief Paul Putzulu, one of the nicest
police officers you'll ever meet, who is absolutely,
positively, nothing like Edmund Chin.*

DEATH ON DIAMOND HEAD

A Kimo Rigg Mystery

by John Madinger

WATERMARK
PUBLISHING

ISBN 978-0-9796769-6-3

Library of Congress Control Number:
2007943260

Design
Leo Gonzalez

Production
Maggie Fujino

Front cover photography
Zak Noyle

Watermark Publishing
1088 Bishop St., Suite 310
Honolulu, Hawaii 96813
Telephone 1-808-587-7766
Toll-free 1-866-900-BOOK
sales@bookshawaii.net
www.bookshawaii.net

Printed in the United States

PART
I

ONE

"**I MIGHT NOT KILL YOU,** you know," he said, smiling at her from behind the smoked-glass lenses. "You never can tell. You might say the one thing that could change my mind."

Stella Roddick was in no position to say anything at the moment, though, the duct tape he'd plastered over her mouth keeping all but muted pleading sounds from escaping. He hadn't spared the tape, either, using the better part of a roll to wrap her up tightly, fastening her down so that nothing moved but those desperate eyes. He thought that part had gone very well, getting behind her, putting her neck in the crook of his arm, cranking up the pressure, feeling her kick and then go limp as the blood quit flowing to her brain. Ease off a bit; don't want her to check out before they had a chance to chat. Then it was as easy as packing her up like today's fresh catch and taking her out to the car. The sushi special of the day, delivered right from your door.

"Do you like sushi?" he said. "Oh, I forgot. The cat's got your tongue. How about if I take that off and we'll see if you can say the one thing that might get you out of this mess. The magic words." He ripped the tape off her mouth and she sucked in two big gulps of air.

"Please don't kill me," she gasped. "Please."

He leaned forward, his face inches from hers. "Aww. And you were so close, too." He slapped the duct tape back over her mouth, muffling her protest. "The magic words were 'Please don't kill him.' That might have done it, you showing me you cared about somebody more than yourself. We'll talk some more in a little while. You and I have got lots to catch up on. Stuff you're gonna be just dying to tell me." He had the filleting knife out now, holding the narrow blade where she could follow it with two terror-filled eyes.

"Those sushi chefs," he said, watching her watch the knife. "They're real artists. I'll bet one of those guys could work on you for three or four hours before you finally died."

She sent a long whine into the duct tape gag, but he didn't seem to hear. He touched the knife to her midriff, bare now, seeing her stomach muscles contracting, trying to pull away.

"Take a little bit here, a little off there. I don't have to tell you. Shoot, you know what I'm talking about. I'm not that good, not enough practice. I'll do the best I can, but I doubt you'll last more than 30, 40 minutes, tops." He looked up at her, killing all but the very last fragment of her hope with his smile. "But hey. Those are gonna be quality minutes for both of us."

Two

IAN RIGG DOUBLE-CHECKED THE DOOR, making sure both of the locks were engaged before turning away from the cottage. Wind sighed through the kiawe trees that covered the seaward end of Diamond Head, a couple of stray branches scratching against the wooden shingles on the side of the house. Down the slope toward Waikiki, a rooster crowed, feeling dawn still an hour away.

Rigg spent 10 minutes of the hour stretching next to the car, loosening up in the dark for the work ahead. At 45, everything took longer and seemed to hurt more. As he finally shook himself out, ready to hit the road, he checked the house again. No sign of anyone stirring yet. At the bottom of the steep driveway, an occasional car flashed past on Diamond Head Road, early-birds heading into Waikiki for a day's work at the hotels.

He took the first leg, an easy grade up past the lighthouse to the lookout, at his warm-up speed, getting into the rhythm of the run; he'd turn up the pace when he got to the plaque marking Amelia Earhart's first solo flight to the mainland. Headlights from behind moved him to the edge of the pavement; always a good idea to leave plenty of room at this hour to a driver who might be drunk or asleep at the wheel. The car slowed as he reached his stride by the monument and didn't pass him. He looked back to check on it, seeing it finishing a U-turn, brake lights flaring as it stopped at the end of the parking area, facing back toward Waikiki.

He picked it up another notch, a full moon hovering over his right shoulder, laying a path of silver on the water below.

Four- or five-foot swells rolled toward the shore, breaking the moonlight into a ladder of light and dark, the foam where the waves broke shining starkly white against the black sea. Rigg thought this was the only time to run. He could cope with the heat and the humidity, but competing with the daytime traffic was another matter. Between gawking tourists and impatient islanders, Honolulu roads could be a minefield for the jogger. At 4:30 a.m. though, he could go for a mile along Kahala Avenue without seeing a car, hearing only the surf grumbling on the distant reef, the slap, slap of his Nikes, and the rasp of his breath in the cool pre-dawn air.

His run this morning was a straight shot down a two-mile gauntlet of multi-million-dollar homes, all the way to the Kahala Hotel, along the golf course and past the mall. Coming back through the neighborhood, he had a decision to make at Kilauea Avenue. Veering right would lead him on a miles-long circuit of the whole of Diamond Head Crater, a long climb and gentle descent, followed by the flat streets of Waikiki, busier by then with early traffic. This morning, with no time to burn and a big day ahead at the office, he stayed left, pushing hard, retracing his steps back up the ocean side of the mountain. This choice led him directly into HPD's crime scene.

He saw the blue flashers, a dozen or more of them, when he reached the top of the hill, the biggest group clustered near his driveway. Slowing to a walk, he waited for the challenge; sooner or later somebody would tell him to stop where he was and probably turn him around. Depending on who did the challenging, Ian Rigg might actually have to do as he was told.

"Police. Hold it right there." The beam hit him full in the face, one of those industrial-strength flashlights favored by HPD and better police departments everywhere. "Shoot. Is that you, Kimo?" The light flicked off. "What the hell you doing out here, this time of morning?"

"Hey, Bucky, howzit?" Rigg said, shaking the offered hand. "Well, I was getting a little exercise, but now I'm just trying to get home."

The patrolman's badge gleamed in the moonlight, the speaker on his portable radio muttering on his shoulder. "Nobody going home that way. We got the road closed, both directions. Where you living now, anyway?"

Road completely closed. Rigg knew what that meant. Somebody was dead or seriously messed up. And from the look of it, it had happened right under his living room window. "I'm renting a place from Mike Stone. Just up the hill from that ambulance." He pointed down the slope. "And my son's home alone. He wakes up and sees all this stuff going on, he's gonna freak out."

"No problem. I'll get on the radio and let 'em know you're coming down."

"Thanks, man. Is it a hit and run, or what?"

"Nah. Homicide for sure. A woman. Looks like they dumped the body off on the side. Pretty bad, I heard."

"Damn. I better check on Kawika. Let 'em know I'm coming, will you?" Rigg accelerated toward the flashing blue strobes and the pool of bright light on the opposite side of the road. Darker shapes moved in between the cars parked haphazardly across Diamond Head Road, passing back and forth in front of the lights. The Crime Scene Unit had arrived, setting up its portable floodlights, the generator already humming.

"Hold up, Kimo." One of the shapes stepped toward him in the road, and Rigg slowed. A man his age in plainclothes with the build of a linebacker, his gold badge hanging from a chain around his neck, stopped at the front of one of the blue-and-white patrol units, leaning on the fender. Detective Calvin Kamaka extended a big hand. "I hear you're coming back to work today. Been too long, probably."

"I'd say 'good morning,' Cal, but if you folks are out working, it probably isn't so good for you or your customer," Rigg said.

Kamaka laughed shortly. "You know what the t-shirt says. 'Homicide. Our day begins when yours ends.'"

"Bucky tell you why I was coming through?"

"He said your house is down there somewhere. Is that right? You living on Diamond Head, now?"

"I just rented a little two-bedroom place from Mike Stone, right there. I've only been here a few days. Haven't even finished moving yet." He pointed up to the house, its rooftop showing above the trees. No lights were burning, so maybe Kawika had managed to sleep through all the commotion. He voiced this thought to Kamaka.

Kamaka squinted up at the cottage, still almost invisible in the growing light. "Can you see anything from up there? That would've been a lucky break."

Rigg shook his head. "No, you can see the road farther down by the lookout, but not this part. The trees screen it out." Then the memory came to him. "Come to think of it though, I did see somebody stopped over here, right when I was starting the run."

"You saw him? What'd he look like?"

"No, not the driver, but the car. I did see the car."

"What kind was it?"

Rigg closed his eyes, trying to picture the car and its U-turn, seeing the brake lights, the shape of the vehicle silhouetted against the kiawe scrub by its headlights. "Boxy. Like a van or an SUV. A van, I think. Light-colored, maybe white. I couldn't see the license plate, but it was mounted on the right. Offset, you know? And the tail lights were rectangles. He came up from the Waikiki side, made a U-turn, and pulled over, right about there." He pointed at the circle of light under the flood lamps, seeing for the first time a pale form lying on the ground in the center. He stared for a few seconds, the déjà vu feeling sweeping over him, lost for a moment in the shock of recognition and the rush and tangle of bad memories.

"What time was it? Kimo? Hey, man."

"Huh? What's that?" Rigg shook himself, dragging his eyes away from the scene.

"What time was this?" Kamaka, who knew those memories, and shared a few, asked patiently.

"Oh. I left the house at 4:15. I probably got down to the street a little before 4:30. A couple of minutes either side."

"Okay. That could be a help. Go on up. Check on your boy. We're definitely gonna want a statement later on, though."

"Shoot, thanks. I'm supposed to meet with the Deputy Chief at nine. I'll come by your office after I get finished."

Kamaka shot him a sympathetic look. "Meeting Chin, huh? That oughta be interesting. Yeah, any time after that's fine."

"You guys are gonna be here awhile," Rigg said over his shoulder. "I'll make up some coffee, bring it down." Kamaka waved.

In the circle of light, one detective in an electric-blue aloha shirt squatted next to the body, everybody else standing 10 or 12 feet away. Rigg recognized him, Jerome Martin, one of the newer of the department's homicide detectives. Martin looked toward him, squinting into the floodlights as Rigg hurried past a patrolman stringing crime scene tape from car to car across the road.

Half an hour later, with the sun up and Kawika perched in the front window, trying to see the action on the street below, Rigg backed out of the front door, a vat of coffee and a pile of cups on a wooden tray. "Get ready for school," Rigg called back into the house. "I'll be right back. You'd better be all set to go when I get here."

At the bottom of the hill, several bystanders, joggers and early morning walkers stood outside the crime scene tape and gazed up toward the medical examiner's station wagon, whispering to each other. Rigg walked up to one of the patrolmen, getting ready to ask him to get Kamaka. Martin saw him first, breaking out of a huddle of four detectives, walking over.

"What the hell is that?" Martin gestured at Rigg's coffee service.

Rigg looked down at the tray and back at Martin like this was a trick question. "Coffee. I figured you guys could use some."

Martin shook his head. "Bringing shit into my crime scene. You oughta know better. And here I thought you knew every damn thing already."

The crime scene techs and a couple of the patrolmen stopped to watch, following the action like a tennis match, waiting now to see what Rigg had to say.

"Jeez, Marty, lighten up. You don't want any coffee, don't take any."

Martin took a step forward, staying on his side of the tape, the line cleanly drawn. "I don't want anything from you. Big whistle-blower hero. You caused nothing but trouble for everybody else. And some of those guys you blew the whistle on had friends. You're out getting rich, they're paying for it."

"That's how it is, huh?"

"You damn right, that's how it is."

Rigg turned his back on the detective, walking over to the side of the road, staying outside the yellow tape. He set the tray down on the low stone wall that served as a guard-rail for Diamond Head Road. "Coffee's here for anybody who wants it," he announced. "Somebody can leave the tray by the mailbox over there, that'd be fine." He looked back once at Martin, who had returned to the body, now covered with a white sheet, then at Kamaka, who shrugged and ducked under the tape, picking up a cup.

"That's how it is, Kimo," Kamaka said.

THREE

THE DESK OF DEPUTY CHIEF of Police Edmund Chin screamed of discipline and control. Everything on it had been carefully chosen after much deliberation, each item making a statement about the man in the high-backed leather chair. In the upper left-hand corner, a brass desk lamp with a green shade and white letters reading "Police" threw soft light onto the polished koa wood. In the opposite corner, a British bobby's helmet sat on a wooden pedestal. A plaque from the Chief Superintendent of New Scotland Yard thanked Chin for his visit. The leather blotter was embossed with the seal of the FBI National Academy, Chin's matching diploma on the wall behind him.

At exactly 10 minutes after nine, having kept his visitor waiting long enough, the Deputy Chief aligned his desk calendar perfectly with the upper right hand corner of the blotter, reaching for the telephone, precisely placed on the corner beneath the lamp.

"You can come in now, Mrs. Tanaka," he said into the speaker.

Opening the folder in front of him, he extracted some papers from the top of the thick pile, swiveling to face away from the door as his two visitors filed in. Ian Rigg and the D.C.'s secretary each took a seat on the other side of the desk, Mrs. Tanaka setting her steno pad and poising her pen. Chin ignored the two of them, apparently absorbed in reading the file. Rigg, who had been in this exact spot several times before, edged his chair a few inches to the left, checked on Mrs. Tanaka, who was gazing out the window, apparently oblivious, then bumped himself a few inches more. The black helmet now obscured about half of the D.C., who was still studying his paper. Although the boss was no longer completely visible, Rigg could see his own name on the top of the sheet in the Deputy's hand.

Rigg joined Mrs. Tanaka in an examination of the buildings of downtown Honolulu through the window, but after a minute or two he reached into his back pocket, pulling out a paperback book. Sliding down in the chair, he opened the book to a marked page, getting about a paragraph done before Chin cleared his throat.

"What are you doing, Sergeant?"

Rigg sat up, keeping at least half of the helmet between him and the Deputy. "Oh. Morning, Chief. I'm just catching up on a little reading for my dissertation." He held up the book. *Discipline and Punish: The Birth of the Prison.* Michel Foucault. French philosopher. Strange guy, but he's got some very interesting theories about the evolution of the power structure of the state. He thinks that rulers don't have to use brute force any more to stay in power. They've replaced violence with other mechanisms for social control, and prisons are the models for disciplinary networks, even a whole disciplined society. You'd appreciate it."

"We're having a meeting, here, Detective." Chin had put the papers down, glaring at Rigg.

Rigg looked over at Mrs. Tanaka, who had dutifully recorded his book report. He thought she might be grinning, ducking her head low over the pad.

"Right, but I thought maybe this part of it was like, you know, Silent Reading Time in kindergarten, when everybody gets to read their own story, only to themselves."

Chin inclined his head to his left to get the helmet completely out of his field of view, Rigg leaning a little harder on his own left arm as Chin stared at him some more, finally closing his eyes and shaking his head, the image of patient forbearance. "No. This is not Silent Reading Time. This is the time we find out what your retirement plans are."

"Sure," Rigg said, carefully re-marking his place in the book. "I've got 22 years on, and I'm planning to go to 30, so eight more years."

A muscle twitched in the Deputy's face, his mouth opening and closing once before he finally got the words out. "Eight years," he said, sounding like somebody had just pronounced sentence on him.

Rigg nodded. "That's the plan," he said brightly. "Of course, I'll only be 53 then, so I might decide to go till 60, see how I feel then, but who knows?"

Chin leaned back in his chair, receding completely out of sight behind the helmet, his disembodied voice tight and edgy. Rigg imagined that somebody had slipped in and now had their hands around Chin's neck, maybe going to throttle him right there in the office. He resisted the urge to lean out and look.

"I can't make you leave, and I can't take you out of Criminal Investigation, the court said so, but that doesn't mean I have to give you anything important to do. So, I'm assigning you to the Unsolved Crimes Section. You'll report to Major Hata in CID. This is the room number for your new office. You'll be down in the basement. Get the key from maintenance." His hand pushed a 3-by-5 card a few inches out from behind the helmet and across the desk, obviously expecting that Rigg would reach forward and pick it up. Since this would, in effect, mean bowing before the Deputy, Rigg left the card where it sat.

"Unsolved Crimes Section, huh? I never heard of it before," Rigg said.

"It's new. A special unit, you might say. In fact, there's only one person assigned there."

"Well, it sounds interesting, not to mention really obvious, but the name makes you wonder; do we have a Solved Crimes Section? That would actually be a lot easier, you know, working on cases that are already solved. I don't imagine there's a lot of 'investigating' to do on those, but think of your clearance rate. I suppose it would be, like, a hundred percent, huh?"

Chin sat up sharply, lunging forward and sweeping the helmet off to the side, the order and correctness of the desk now irretrievably violated. They could see each other clearly now, though. Rigg thought the effort needed to prevent an explosion was starting to show, signs of stress popping out all over.

"No," Chin said through teeth tightly clenched. "We don't have a section for that. It's a thought, though." He fumbled for his pen and made a small note on Rigg's file folder, trying to recover some composure.

"What kinds of crimes, exactly, does 'Unsolved Crimes' solve?" Rigg said.

"Anything Major Hata decides to assign you. I'm sure he'll find something … suitable."

"Anything from lost dogs to serial killers, eh?"

Chin smiled, one corner of his grin noticeably higher than the other, a canine tooth showing, the strain definitely taking a toll on the calm façade. "Oh, I don't expect you'll be getting any homicides. We have real detectives for those. Good ones." Leaving Rigg no doubt where he stood in the batting order.

"Well, I guess I don't have any choice," Rigg said. "It sounds like you've met the terms of the settlement agreement, and I know you wouldn't want to do anything to get the judge any madder at you than he already was."

Chin flinched visibly at the mention of the judge, probably remembering the monumental ass-chewing he'd taken down at the federal courthouse two months ago.

"You have a choice. You could retire," he said hopefully.

"No, no, I wouldn't think of quitting now. I'll give this special unit section thing a shot. Who knows? The whole deal could turn out okay." Rigg slapped the book against his leg, causing Mrs. Tanaka to jump in her seat. "Detectives, unsolved crimes, what a concept! It might be me, but it sounds just crazy enough to work! I'm excited to be a part of it."

His face quivering noticeably and sweat beading on his forehead, Chin tried again for a smile, found the effort too great and gave up. "We're finished, then. Check in with Major Hata." He picked up the papers again, an obvious dismissal.

Rigg stood with Mrs. Tanaka, collecting the index card from the desk and waiting for her to leave ahead of him, the official record of the meeting now closed. He stopped in the doorway. "Say, Chief, I was wondering," he said.

Chin looked up, frowning. "What is it, now?"

"I guess since we skipped Silent Reading Time and went straight to 'go to the time out corner,' that means we're not having juice and snack today, huh?"

"Get out," Chin screamed, losing it at last. "And don't come back."

FOUR

THE DOOR YIELDED RELUCTANTLY, swinging into the darkness on hinges creaky from neglect. Rigg groped for the light switch on the wall, rewarded with a flicker and then the cold glow of fluorescence cascading down onto the three metal desks. The maintenance man stopped in the doorway, both of them taking in the crowded little room.

"This sucks," he said to the maintenance man, who shrugged.

"You're lucky. Down the hall in Vice, they got three guys sharing one desk. In here, you got three desks for one guy. Go figger."

"Yeah, I'm feeling lucky, all right. Do those things work?" Rigg pointed at an HPD computer terminal, scanner and printer sitting on the farthest desk.

"Supposed to. The computer people was in here Friday, had that stuff on, hooked up the phone, too."

Rigg took note of the single telephone, a set of phone books, internal and external, and the thick HPD Operations Manual. Other than these items, the room was empty. "I'd say it's about perfect for mushroom cultivation or meat storage."

"Huh?" the maintenance man said.

Rigg waved it off. "Nothing. Is it always this cold down here?"

"Yep. Can't do nothin' about that. Best bring a sweater."

"Wasn't this a storeroom or something before?"

"Yep. Narco kept their stuff in here. You done somethin' to piss somebody off," the maintenance man accused. "Must've been big."

"I won a million bucks from the Deputy Chief," Rigg said. "That's pretty big. And yeah, I think he's still pissed about it."

The maintenance man pointed. "You're him. You're the one."

"Yes, well, judging by my luxurious new surroundings, some people apparently think so," Rigg said.

"I gotta go," the maintenance man said, vanishing into the hallway before Rigg could thank him for the key.

He tossed *Discipline and Punish: The Birth of the Prison* onto the nearest desk. "Tell you one thing," he said to the bare walls. "Ol' Foucault would have had some stuff to say about this place."

The computer could wait, he thought; he needed to deal with other pressing administrative matters. Like getting a place for his car in a building where parking was always at a premium. This meant going upstairs to the Administrative Bureau, which meant Iwa.

Iwalani Hu, actually Lieutenant Iwalani Hu, and Ian James Rigg went way, way back. They had lived across the street from each other, and her older brother David, exactly Rigg's age, had been an early partner in mischief, if not crime. When the time came for intermediate school, the boys were separated for the first time, David's parents sending him to Kamehameha, and the Riggs sending their son down the valley to Punahou. Kamehameha had accepted Rigg, too, and he'd argued vehemently for the chance to stay with his friend. "Ha. You know what 'kolohe' means?" his mother, herself a Kamehameha alumna had asked. "Rascal," he told her. "That's right. And the two of you together would be the biggest kolohe in the history of the Kamehameha Schools," she said. "Princess Pauahi would never forgive me." The judgment delivered, the two of them wound up competing on the baseball and football fields, rascality confined by parental power to evenings, week-ends and long, languid Manoa summers.

Iwa, four years younger, had been an irritant and an unwanted tag-along, easily outdistanced, but never per-manently lost. And she had bestowed on Rigg one of those younger-sister crushes that burn more fiercely and generally crush more completely than other forms of teenage passion. When it came time for her to leave elementary school, she'd begged successfully for the chance to follow him to Punahou, Rigg taking plenty of ribbing from David and his school friends about the gawky seventh-grader who mooned at him in the cafeteria and came to every game.

There was nothing gawky about Iwalani Hu these days. She'd changed a lot, undergoing one of those magical duck-ling-to-swan transformations that take the breath away and leave even an older brother's best friend struck dumb. She was very simply the most beautiful woman Rigg had ever known, and unlike most crushes, Iwalani's hadn't faded. She'd joined the police department six years after Rigg, looking for a chance to let him know she still remembered and still cared as she climbed HPD's ladder. She'd finally caught him at the right moment in the middle of his long trial with Ed Chin, when his wife had moved out and all his confidence had drained away. The result had been confusing, at least for Rigg, who told Iwa one night, "It's like going into the wrong house and finding yourself at home."

"Turn off the light," she said. "You've been home all along."

At the counter in Admin, one of the clerks, a cute Filipino girl, gave him a new building pass like she was bestowing the Medal of Honor, fussing over him and writing her name, her office extension and her home number on the form that went with the parking place in the basement. "Angelina Flores, just in case you've got any questions," she said. He stood there contemplating his newfound popularity when Iwa's voice came from behind him. "Well, look what sergeant the cat dragged in."

He gave her a hug, complimented her on the new gold kukui nuts that HPD uses to display lieutenants' rank, and followed her into her office, taking a seat in front of a desk covered six inches deep in paper, and showing her the parking form and her employee's numbers. "What's that all about?" he said.

"Are you kidding? You've got a million dollars and a red Porsche. She's a Clerk II. What do you think it's all about?"

"Oh. I thought maybe it was my animal magnetism," he said, trying to sound disappointed.

"Let me take care of that for you," she said, taking the paper and vigorously scratching out the numbers. "Animal magnetism. You have any questions, you know who to call."

"How's Kawika?" they both said together, the two of them laughing.

"Mine's doing good," Rigg said. "He thinks he's going to be the next Tiger Woods. I'm just glad he doesn't want to try football. His size, he'd get creamed." Rigg thought that his Kawika, named after Iwa's brother, might eventually end up taller, but he hadn't started filling out yet. "How's yours?"

"He's fine," Iwa said. "In Afghanistan somewhere, doing something dangerous." Colonel David "Kawika" Hu had gone from Kamehameha's ROTC program to the Naval Academy, then into the Marine Corps, seeing action in both of America's Middle East wars, back there now for a new helping. "I heard from him a week ago," she said.

"Yeah, me too," Rigg said. "He never says much in those emails. Leaves too much to the imagination, you ask me."

"Are you really back? I saw the paperwork," she said,

picking up a pencil and spinning it. "You're not going to take the money and run?"

"Nah. It's never been about the money for me. I'm happy doing the job."

"You've got to be realistic, Kimo. They're never going to give you the chance to be happy here again."

"I'm starting to figure that out."

"Maybe you should look at the state. They've got the same benefits we do. We lose about five or six people a year to them, mostly folks close to retirement."

"I'll think about it," Rigg said. "But I don't want to get too far away from my guardian angel. Especially now that she's a lieutenant."

She smiled. "Who knows? I might follow you over there."

"It's happened before," he said. "And hey, now I've got a red Porsche and a million bucks."

She flipped the pencil at him. "You better remember, buddy," she said, dropping her voice, "who loved you before you were rich and famous."

FIVE

AFTER SITTING AROUND in his new office for an hour trying to make the phone and the computer work, Rigg headed back upstairs to CID. He needed to check in with the major, and he wanted to give Kamaka the one-page memo he'd written on the morning's activity at his house. This plan quickly ran into problems.

"Access Denied," said the little message on the card reader next to the door at CID. He tried his new building pass card again. Same result. He pushed the button on the speakerphone.

"Amy, this is Kimo Rigg. Buzz me in, will you? My card's not working."

There was a long pause. He was just getting ready to push the button again when the box beeped. "He's not in, Kimo."

What the hell? He pushed the button. "Who's not in?"

Another pause. "Major Hata says ... I mean, the major's in a meeting. I mean *at* a meeting ... Somewhere else."

Rigg stared at the box, then up at the camera on the wall. He wondered whether he should push the button again. He wondered if he should give up and go away. He wondered if the idiot and his bobby hat on the fourth floor had decided to go for double or nothing. He pushed the button.

"Okay, then. I've got a report for Kamaka. Is he in a meeting?"

The speakerphone thought this one over for what seemed like a very long time. "Can you slide it under the door?" it finally said.

Fortunately for the door, the speakerphone and Ian Rigg, Cal Kamaka walked up behind Rigg, carding the door, which snapped open immediately. "Hi, Kimo," Cal said. "You coming to see me? Hey, you look a little red. You get too much sun yesterday?"

A clutch of three clerical people, eyes as big and shiny as compact discs, stood next to the intercom box and the TV monitor, watching Rigg and Kamaka come down the hallway. Two of them slunk away, leaving Amy Fraga, the receptionist, looking especially mortified, holding both hands over her mouth, trying to hide the source of the words she'd just spoken.

Rigg stood in front of her while Kamaka walked over to the mailboxes for his messages, reading one as he came back.

"Slide it under the door, Amy?" Rigg said, shaking his head and turning with Kamaka toward the Homicide office.

"What was that all about?" Kamaka said, looking back over his shoulder.

"Nothing. I've gotta talk to the major later. He's at a meeting. Somewhere else."

"No, he's not. He was talking on his phone when I went by his office."

"Hell with it. It can wait. I wanted to give you my memo from this morning. I haven't figured out how to make the email work on my new computer yet."

"Oh, you got a new assignment, eh? Where are you gonna be? Everybody was guessing where they'd put you. I said Narco."

"You were close, at least geographically. I'm in the Unsolved Crimes Section. It's a special unit. In the basement."

Kamaka looked surprised. "Unsolved Crimes Section? What the hell is that?"

"I dunno for sure, Cal. But I'd say it's the hole they'd like to bury me in."

They reached the Homicide office, Kamaka carding the door. "You gotta hang in there. They can't run you off now."

"Oh, they're not stupid enough to try and run me off. They went that route once and it cost Chin a million bucks. No, they want me to get fed up and leave."

"Well, you can't let them do that, either."

Rigg thought about locks that wouldn't open, people who weren't in but were, and reports delivered through cracks under doors. "I don't know. This crap could get pretty old, pretty fast," he said.

Kamaka read through Rigg's report, asked a couple of questions, then dropped the paper off to the side of his desk, the two of them looking at each other in silence, each waiting for the other to speak first.

"I know what you're thinking," Kamaka said finally. "But you're wrong this time."

"You know what I'm thinking, that means you've been thinking the same thing," Rigg said. "How come you're so sure I'm wrong?"

"Because the man is dead, that's why. This is a coincidence."

"C'mon, Cal. Since when did you start believing in coincidences in murder investigations? Especially in this case. I couldn't see much this morning, but I saw enough. She was laid out just like the others. He parked her about 50 yards from the ocean. And if I'm not mistaken, that was a white van I saw this morning. Sounds like the coincidences are starting to mount up. There's something else, isn't there?"

Kamaka looked away. "All that stuff was in the papers. Everybody in Honolulu knew we were looking for a white van. All the bodies were dumped near water. Even the double cross thing, must be hundreds of people knew about that, thousands, maybe. You know how it is in this town, everybody talks. And the bottom line is, the guy's dead, so it couldn't be."

"He crossed her feet at the ankles and her hands over her head." Rigg said. "Just like the others. And this one was cut, too," he guessed.

Kamaka didn't say anything.

"Okay. So, another coincidence. That's four. She looked like a haole girl, with brown hair. That would be five and six."

Kamaka didn't say anything.

"She was nude, and he dumped her in the early morning. Jeez, man, we're almost into double figures, here."

"There's some big differences, though," Kamaka said. "This one was way older. Around 30. The Double-crosser never took anybody over 20. Plus, the wounds are different. Not as many. Not as … vicious."

Rigg looked at him, waiting for the bottom line. Kamaka wasn't ready to give it up just yet.

"He's dead, Kimo. We had the right guy, you know we did. And he's dead. It cannot be."

"What about the feet?"

Kamaka looked away again.

"Jesus Christ," Rigg breathed. "That was the one thing we held like gold. We were even bagging the hands and feet before the paramedics got to them, hell, before even the ME's people saw them. How many people knew about that? Even on the task force, we didn't tell everybody. Only a few of us and the killer knew that. We let everybody think he was called the Double-crosser because of the arrangement of the body, not the cuts on the feet."

"Yeah, but even that was different this time. This time the wounds were post mortem. And he didn't really slice her up like the Double-crosser used to. It looks like she just got one stab, straight to the heart. The M.O.'s not the same at all."

"What M.O.'s not the same?" Jerome Martin stood over

them, a stack of evidence envelopes in his hands. "You're not cutting up my case with this civilian, are you, Cal? I wouldn't like that."

"Hey, Marty," Rigg said. "No, we were talking about one of my old cases. And you obviously didn't hear the news. I'm back working again. Right here in CID."

"Big whoop," Martin said. "Just goes to show how screwed up the brass is. Any of 'em had any balls, you'd be a floorwalker down at Macy's Ala Moana."

"No, I did way better than that. I'm lead detective in the Unsolved Crimes Section. It's a special unit. In the basement. Sorry, but I can't tell you any more than that."

Martin gaped at him. "There's no 'Special Unsolved Crimes Section.'" He looked at Kamaka, who shrugged.

"There is now. It's an exciting concept," Rigg said. "We're employing some of Michel Foucault's pioneering ideas on the role of surveillance in promoting voluntary discipline in the individual. I probably shouldn't have told you that."

"You're fuckin' nuts, you know that? Surveillance. Voluntary discipline. I can't believe you're hanging out with this guy," Martin said to Kamaka. Shaking his head, he turned toward his desk as Rigg stood up to leave.

"Oh, and Marty." Martin came around slowly. "For your information, at least one of the brass did have some balls once, but thanks to Judge Klein down at federal court, I've got them now in a frame on my wall. Come down to the basement one day and check it out." Rigg started for the door. "Bring a magnifying glass, though, 'cause they're really, really, teeny."

Six

AT THE RECEPTION DESK, Amy Fraga stood when Rigg walked up. "Kimo," she said, "I … I didn't mean …"

"Never mind. It's not your fault. Is he back from his meeting?"

She nodded, silently mouthing "I'm so sorry," as he headed for the major's office.

Major Richard Hata, "Rick" to Rigg since their academy days, glanced up from the reports on his desk, double-taking when he saw who it was. Rigg walked directly in.

"Your meeting over?" he said.

Hata nodded. "Come on in, Kimo. Sit down."

"No, I'll stand. I don't want to hang out somewhere I'm not wanted. But I've gotta tell you, we need to nip this thing in the bud, right now. This is the only time I'm gonna say this. I'm not gonna wave the freakin' judgment around every time something I don't like goes down around here. But I can tell you, if I go to Mike Stone with what just happened out there, he's gonna land on you like a 747. The judge said no more retaliation, and he meant it."

"We can explain that."

"You probably can. It's my first day back. The card didn't work. You were going to a real meeting. Whatever. The point is, the two of us, we're starting down the road, here. I've already seen what's at the end, and I'm telling you as a friend, I don't think you want to go there."

The major leaned back in his chair, looking up at the ceiling. "You might be right," he said.

"We go back a long way. You're nobody's fool, Rick.

Don't be somebody's tool."

Hata nodded, maybe giving in.

"Enough about that," Rigg said. "That thing this morning was just a snafu. Could've happened to anybody. Forget it. So, tell me what unsolved crime the Unsolved Crimes Section is supposed to solve."

Hata didn't answer immediately, and didn't meet Rigg's eyes when he finally did. "Tagging," he said sheepishly.

Rigg wasn't expecting that. "*Tagging*? You're gonna put me on graffiti patrol? Have me stake out some freeway sign, see if I can catch some juvie tagging it?"

"Not for a week. Then I'm supposed to give you the assignment."

Rigg shook his head, disbelieving. "Amazing. So, I'm supposed to sit down there in my cave for a week, twiddling my thumbs until you can drop this on me? Is that it?"

"It's not like I want to do this."

"Yeah, that's what the last guy said, too. Look what it got him. Where is Captain Lopaki now? Oh, yeah. Lieutenant Lopaki's supervising the 9-1-1 operators on the midnight watch," Rigg said. "Okay. Here's how I want to play this. If you can't live with it, tell me right now and I'll call Mike, start the ball rolling down at the courthouse. First, I want my freakin' building pass to work in the card readers. No more of this 'access denied' shit. Second, I don't want you poking Amy or anybody else out front. According to Chin, I'm supposed to be reporting to you. Fine. You got something you want to say to me, come out and say it. We're both big kids, I can take whatever it is." Rigg took a deep breath. "And third, I want the Double-crosser file sent down to my office."

He might have seen the first two coming, but the last request took Hata by surprise. "You're thinking about that thing this morning. Martin's case."

"No, the Double-crosser was mine, or at least the task force's. Martin didn't work it. He was still in Patrol then. I don't want anything to do with Marty's murder; I just want to go through the old reports. And I've got a whole week with nothing else to do, so it works out perfectly."

"There's 30 boxes in that file."

"Thirty-two, I think. Don't worry, I got lots of room down there, once I get rid of two of those damn desks."

Hata thought about it for a minute. "He's got you in the old Narco storeroom, doesn't he?"

"Yeah. But it could've been worse. It might've been a stall in the men's john."

Hata laughed. "Okay, I'll fix the other stuff. I can't do anything about the graffiti job, though. Chin ran it by Counsel's office already and they say it's a real criminal investigation, so it meets the terms of the settlement agreement. You're just going to have to suck it up on that one, but if you need something else, let me know."

"What about the file?"

The major reached for his telephone. "Last I heard, Records had it stored off-site. They were complaining about the cost, since it's a closed case and there's no way to prosecute now that the suspect's dead. They'll be happy to know there's some free storage space, just came open down in the basement."

SEVEN

"DRUG ENFORCEMENT, SILAFAU."

"Nate, this is Kimo."

"Kimo! You back at work? Shoot, I can't believe it."

"I'm back. It's been a trip."

"Can you get away for lunch, or are you too busy already?"

Rigg thought about the delayed onset of his big tagging case, the week or more he had waiting for him in the basement. "Lunch won't be a problem," he said.

They met at one of their usual spots, a Chinese restaurant off Hotel Street downtown. Nate Silafau, a Special Agent with the Drug Enforcement Administration, had worked for five years with Rigg on a DEA-HPD task force, a period both of them still thought of as a high point in their careers.

Rigg parked two blocks away, walking to the restaurant past the eclectic mix of art galleries and peep shows, open-air lei stands and Chinese herb shops that made Honolulu's Chinatown such a joy in the daytime. The same streets took on a whole different complexion at night, though, when the transvestite hookers and the jack-rollers were out, the meth salesmen and the junkies hanging in every shuttered doorway, the glow from their ice pipes and their cigarettes little warning lights in the darkness.

Silafau got to the restaurant first, walking over from the federal building, but he hadn't gone in yet, talking in animated Samoan to one of the hangers-on outside a video store across the street. From the look of it, the DEA agent was giving the man a serious dressing down.

"What were you doing out there?" Rigg asked when Silafau came in and sat down.

"Ahh, I promised his mom I'd keep an eye on him, and there he is, strong-arming for somebody's gambling game. I told him, I see him out here again after today, he's gonna get his ass kicked."

Rigg leaned out and peered through the flyspecked window at the hulking enforcer, now studiously avoiding looking in their direction.

"How exactly are you gonna pull that off? That guy's got you by eight inches at least, and he must outweigh you by a 150 pounds."

"I'm not gonna do it myself, smartass. I ain't crazy. I tell his mama, she'll whip his ass but good. She might not be as tall, but she's got him by 50 pounds herself."

Nate Silafau, known affectionately in Hawaii law enforcement circles as "the world's smallest Samoan," was also a member of one of the leading families in Samoa, hence his other nickname, "Prince." With the title came the responsibility for looking after members of Hawaii's Samoan community. He got four or five requests a week for some favor or other. Only half-Samoan, he'd inherited his haole mother's size, topping out at six inches over five feet, almost a foot shorter than many of the crooks he locked up. It was a common sight in federal court to see a prayer circle of towering Polynesians, the defendant's family, and sometimes his rugby teammates, all with heads bowed so they could see the diminutive Silafau, all listening respectfully while Nate explained the bail arrangements or the charges in Samoan.

"Tagging? You're gonna be going after graffiti? You've gotta be kidding," Silafau said after they ordered.

"I wish I was kidding, but at least it doesn't start right away," Rigg said. "They're gonna surprise me with it next week.

In the meantime, I've got to find some unsolved crimes of my own."

"I know where there's a gambling game going on, got strong-arm protection," Silafau said, aiming his chopsticks across the street. "You could solve that one pretty quick. I could probably even get you an informant."

Rigg laughed. "Thanks, but I'll let Vice take it. I don't want to step on any more toes down there for a while."

"How's the reception been?"

"Mixed. Most people seem okay. Some are still pissed off. And some just don't want to get too close to me, think I might have something catching. I got a little of all three today."

"How many years you have, yet?"

"I told Chin eight, but I don't know if I can make it that long. Or want to."

"Mmm. Eight years. That'd be a long time, chasing graffiti artists."

Rigg had to agree. "It's not all bad, though. I've got a parking space right outside the office in the basement. Plus, I've got to be the only police in Honolulu with his very own secret underground lair. I can emerge from the cave, climb into the car, go forth to crush some crime. Well, at least some taggers. How could it be any better?"

Silafau cocked his head. "Secret underground lair?"

"Yeah, and you know what I really need? I need to borrow that Samoan fruit bat you've got on the plaque behind your desk. That's just the decorative accent that would make it perfect."

"Seriously?"

"Hell, yes. If I've got to climb into that hole every day, I'm at least going to fix it up so it's comfortable down there. Nobody said I couldn't."

"Did you drive the new car in to the office?" Silafau said.

A car buff with contacts in every dealership on the island, it was Silafau who had talked Rigg into spending some of his settlement on new wheels, a 20-year-old Porsche 930 Turbo. "You know you've always wanted a Porsche," Silafau had told him. "And I can get you a great deal."

The car, bright red, insanely fast and full of what Rigg called "Porsche problems, lots and lots of little things that all cost big money to fix," hadn't actually set him back much more than a new SUV, but it looked much cooler and definitely made a statement at the station.

"Yeah, it's parked a couple of blocks over," Rigg said. "I'll give you a ride back when we're done. It's popular with the clerical people, anyway."

"Did you get the vanity plates yet?"

"No, it takes a couple of weeks."

"Hoo boy, Chin's gonna spit nails when he sees that," Silafau chortled.

"He parks a level up, but the word'll get back. You know cops, we love to talk."

They ate their noodles and fried rice and talked about happenings at the federal building, where the never-ending wars between the various federal agencies always provided good gossip. When they were about finished, Rigg brought up the murder, wanting to bounce some ideas off his old partner.

"I'm taking a look at the Double-crosser case again. Homicide got a body this morning on Diamond Head Road, right down from my house. The similarities are spooky. A ton of coincidences."

"Probably a copycat. That case made the front page for weeks. Plenty of sickos out there, would love to see their crime get that kind of attention." There had never been a drug angle, so Silafau hadn't worked the Double-crosser, but he'd kept up on the case through Rigg and the other detectives.

"Could be. But whoever did this one knew something only a couple of people knew. Basically just a few detectives, the ME, the Deputy Prosecutor and the killer."

"One thing's for sure, it can't be the original Double-crosser. He's dead, or at least that's what everybody says," Silafau said. "And there haven't been any more killings for what? Four years?"

"Four years almost exactly," Rigg said.

"So, if it can't be the guy—what was his name?"

"Streck. Ray Streck."

"Yeah, so if it can't be him for this one, it's gotta be a copycat. You sure you had the right guy the first time?"

"I was until about 5:30 this morning. The evidence was strong against Streck. He drove a white van, and we got victim DNA out of it, got a knife from his house that could've been used. He had a collection of news articles on the cases in his bedroom. There were even Polaroids of one of the girls, the last one, tied up in the van. Plus, we got a DNA match for Streck on one of the victims. He was a perfect fit."

"What did the FBI say?"

"The behavioral science guys saw it as a lone-wolf. We sent the details from each killing up to Washington and they came up with a pretty good profile. They called him an 'organized serial killer.' According to them, we were looking for somebody who targeted strangers, used restraints—the Double-crosser duct-taped everybody—and had a controlled crime scene."

Rigg looked out the window again, watching the Samoan strong-arm let a couple of women through the door. They looked like Korean bar hostesses, out to lose their money on video poker. "We never actually found the crime scene. Most of us thought it was probably the van. He got the women, and once they were in the van, they never left it alive.

"Anyway, Streck matched up almost perfectly with the profile. They said our boy would be socially competent, which Streck was. He had a job doing deliveries, that's what the van was for. They liked him at work. He did okay with women. That was one thing they got wrong on the profile, though."

"What's that?"

"Oh, they said he'd be living with someone, he wouldn't be alone. But Streck had been living by himself for a year after his wife left him."

"Why'd she leave? She find out he was Jack the Ripper disguised?"

"Nah, she met some guy at her work, her boss, I think, and they hit it off. He got some management job in California, a promotion, and she quit and went with him. I went up to L.A. and interviewed her. She basically said Ray was a loser and wasn't going anywhere, and she wanted something better than a delivery boy. Said she told him that, too, before she left."

"Ouch," Silafau laughed. "That could set you off."

"Maybe," Rigg said. "Something sure did. And the FBI said he'd be above average intelligence, below average in empathy. That's pretty obvious, huh? The guy kills eight women that we know of and somebody says he's under-stocked in the empathy department."

"Famous But Incompetent," Silafau said. "They get stuff wrong all the time, but their profilers are supposed to be the best."

"We bought into it. I think we wanted to. When Streck died, the killings stopped; that's pretty conclusive. And when you factor in the evidence we got after he died, well, everybody figured, that's it."

Silafau stood up. "I gotta get back. But it sounds to me like if the killings stopped when the suspect died, it's case closed, crime solved."

Rigg tossed the tip onto the table. "Yeah. I've spent the last four years thinking that exact same thing. I wish I was still as sure as I was last night."

"So, is the Special Unsolved Crimes Section gonna try and solve this one?" Silafau said.

"S-U-C-S. 'Sucks,' huh? It does sort of sum things up down in the basement," Rigg laughed. "No, I'm just going through the old files, see what turns up. I don't know if I'll have the free time anyway, what with all those badass graffiti artists to run down."

Two hours later, back in his secret underground lair, Rigg's phone rang. "SUCS, this is Detective Rigg," he said.

"Sucks, huh? I'll bet it does," Cal Kamaka laughed. "I'll tell you what sucks. It took me 10 minutes to find somebody who knew your phone number."

"It's probably classified top secret. You're my first call."

"Yeah? Well, this is a top secret. I found another coincidence for you," Kamaka said. "You ain't gonna believe this one. We just identified the body from this morning. Her prints were on file."

"Who was she?"

"Stella Roddick. I don't know why I didn't recognize her right off, but I thought you'd want to know."

"Holy shit," Rigg said.

EIGHT

STELLA RODDICK. The witness who tipped them to Ray Streck. He didn't need the old files to bring back the Stella memories. Everybody on the task force remembered how the case had turned around. She hadn't dialed the task force's hotline, instead calling Crimestoppers, the number out there for crime tips of all sorts. Those calls went straight to a recording, and you didn't have to leave your name or number unless you thought you might want a reward, but Stella had left a fake name and a cell phone number.

Stella's first call was bare bones; she'd seen a white van in a townhouse condo parking lot in Kaneohe, across the mountains from Honolulu. She said she thought the owner was suspicious and gave Streck's name. The Crimestoppers clerk took the information off the recorder and sent it to Narcotics, since half or more of the incoming tips had something to do with drugs and a quick check of Streck's rap sheet showed a conviction years before for marijuana sales.

With about zillion similar tips already stacked up, Narcotics put this one at the bottom of the pile, which meant they'd get around to calling Stella back about Ray Streck in around 2020. The next day, Stella phoned again, wanting to know why nobody had called her, mentioning for the first time the series of killings that had the whole town in an uproar. That got the message routed to the task force, which also had a zillion tips about white vans or suspicious men, but had enough people to work every one of them within a couple days of the time they came in. The detective who got the message decided Streck fit parts of the FBI's profile, thinking maybe he would be worth a closer look, and he did some basic background checks, which made Ray Streck look better all the time. Streck was in his late 20s and drove a white delivery van. His physical description also matched that provided by the only eyewitness to one of the abductions, the kidnapping and murder of Amber Wheatley, Double-crosser victim number two.

Amber had been stopped with a flat on the Pali Highway when the eyewitness drove past. The witness knew Amber and knew her car, so he'd slowed, was going to stop and give her a hand, when he saw the man stand up with the flat he'd just taken off the car. It was raining fairly heavily, and deciding she had enough help already, the witness headed for home. When he saw Amber's car still there on his morning commute the next day, he called the police. Amber turned up a day after that, laid out on the edge of Keehi Lagoon by the Honolulu airport, her hands and feet crossed like the first girl, sending the Police Department into a full-blown crisis and an all-out hunt.

They were looking, according to the eyewitness, for a white male, in his late 20s or early 30s, driving a white van that had been parked in front of Amber's car. He might have been big, but the witness only saw him as he was bending over the trunk, a tire in his arms. He might have had brown hair or maybe black, but the witness couldn't be sure; he'd been traveling 50 mph in the rain at the time.

Appeals for other drivers to call in if they'd seen anything that day brought a smattering of tips, but nothing better than the original witness. After the task force detective checked out Streck based on Stella's call, they went back to Amber Wheatley's friend, this time taking pictures of Ray Streck. He could've been the one, the witness said, or maybe not.

When the task force detective called her back on the cell phone, she still wouldn't give her name but now she was fishing for a piece of the reward. A total of $159,000 had been gathered from various sources, the money to be paid "for information leading to the identification, arrest, etc. ..." Stella wanted to know if she could still collect on it now that Streck was dead.

He had died of an overdose in his house, she said. The paramedics had been there and taken him away the day before but she heard he wasn't coming back. His van was still parked in front of his condo, she could see it from her window.

The detective didn't tell Stella that they'd already started looking at Streck, but pumped her for enough information to get a search warrant for the van, holding out the prospect of some of the reward if he actually turned out to be the guilty party. She told him she'd seen the van gone on two nights in particular when murders had taken place, and seen Streck, who worked on his delivery job during the daytime, coming home early in the morning on several other occasions. Stella still didn't want to give her real name, but she said she'd call back.

By eliminating other residents in the townhouse complex, they narrowed the search for their witness to S. Roddick, who lived in the townhouse across the parking lot from Streck. She was no cherry, having been convicted once for check fraud six years earlier. Rigg liked that. She'd been in the system before, somebody who knew something suspicious when she saw it. She lived alone, although the neighbors said she'd had a boyfriend before that they hadn't seen around for a while. On the afternoon they did the search of the van, Rigg and another detective had gone door to door in the complex, making a big deal about talking to residents, making sure Stella would see it. When they finally got to her door, she told them she was the one who'd called and she wanted the reward if anybody was going to get it.

Rigg couldn't remember whether Stella had ever gotten

the money she'd been looking for, but they definitely wouldn't have been able to pin the killings on Streck without her calls. When the search of the van turned up evidence from the killings, they'd gotten another warrant for Streck's townhouse, scoring more evidence of his connection to the Double-crosser's crimes. The Chief disbanded the task force a week later, three detectives from Homicide staying on to wrap up the loose ends, and the others, Rigg included, going back to their previous assignments. Case closed, suspect not prosecutable. They resigned themselves to letting God do the judging on Ray Streck, and so it had stayed for four years.

After Kamaka's call, and still in a state of shock at the news, he got on the computer and ran Stella Roddick, pulling up all the information the department had on the woman and her activities over the past four years, printing it all out. She'd had some more trouble, an arrest for theft and a traffic accident in Kaneohe only a couple of months before. The police report said she was unemployed at the time of the accident, and she had no insurance, which got her a ticket even though the wreck hadn't been her fault. She had a new address on Date Street, a not-especially-distinguished part of Honolulu, and a 10-year-old Toyota registered in her name. It didn't look like Stella had won the lottery or married big money before she got dumped on Diamond Head Road that morning.

At 2:00 and with nothing else to do, Rigg decided to see if he could get rid of a couple of the desks, give himself a little more room to move around the cave. He found a willing taker right next door. Captain Carvalho from Narcotics was happy to get them back.

"Chin took 'em away from us last week, told us to move them next door," the Captain said. "We lost the storage room and the desks, too. At least we get the desks back. How do you want to handle it on the inventory?"

"Inventory?"

"Yeah. They must be assigned to you. You're the unit commander. Did you sign for everything in the office on the equipment inventory?" Carvalho said.

"No, I didn't sign anything. And it's just me. They're not putting anybody else over here."

"So, officially, they're still on my inventory. I don't think we took them off."

"They're not mine, and I don't want 'em, so I'll tell you what, we'll record the numbers, you take them back, and if anybody ever asks where they are, we can move them right back here." Rigg said. "In fact, take all three of 'em. I'm gonna get a new one. Maybe bring one from home."

With the desks gone, the store room felt a lot roomier, and Rigg considered where he wanted to keep the Double-crosser boxes. At quitting time he went next door to the Scandinavian furniture store and ordered a teak desk, a matching credenza, a new rug, and a leather recliner. The office spruce-up would commence tomorrow.

NINE

ALONG WAIKIKI'S ALA WAI CANAL, Honolulu's outrigger canoe clubs keep their six-man practice boats lined up in neat rows at the water's edge. You wouldn't want to swim in the Ala Wai, but its calm waters and access to the ocean make it an ideal training area for the paddlers of canoes and kayaks. Every afternoon, dozens of crews, adults and teenagers, are on the canal, the racing canoes zipping along the smooth surface, doing flat-water sprints or paddling toward the Ala Wai boat harbor and the Pacific beyond.

Rigg's club met by the Waikiki library, more than a mile from the harbor entrance, the senior men and some of the youth teams crewing the boats on Mondays, Wednesdays and Fridays. He'd had plenty of time for paddling practice recently, his administrative leave from the department stretching endlessly from day to day and then month to month.

Kawika's crew also trained on Rigg's days, the kids chattering happily as they launched their boats into the sluggish current. Rigg watched as the boys' coach settled Kawika's crew to the job at hand, and then called his own crew around to go over the day's practice routine. "We'll warm up down to the first bridge, then pick it up to the harbor entrance, then pound it out down to Diamond Head, see how long that takes us," he told them.

Hawaiian outrigger canoes have six seats, the paddler in each seat having a role to play on the team. The first seat, in the bow, sets the pace for the boat while the second seat, behind him, calls all the paddling changes, usually 15 strokes on one side, then "hut" and "ho," and all of the paddlers, who alternate left and right sides, shift their paddles to the opposite side of the boat.

The third and fourth seats are power positions, the motor that drives the boat. Some crews also put a strong paddler in seat five, normally a place for a utility man who keeps the rhythm and works with the rest of the boat. In Rigg's boat, seat five held Barry "Bear" Akana, a supervisor with the state's Adult Probation Division. The steersman and boat captain occupies the last seat, guiding the canoe with a large steering paddle and stroking whenever he's able. Good steersmen paddle almost as much as the rest of the crew, making the small course corrections and adjustments necessary to trim the boat and guide it to the conditions most favorable on the race course.

At 5'10", and not one of the larger paddlers, Rigg did the steering for his crew, spending the entire session watching the wind and the waves, the paddlers and the racecourse over Bear's broad shoulders. This afternoon, he took them out of the Ala Wai, turning left for a long upwind pull up to the Diamond Head buoy, back down almost to Honolulu harbor, then a final sprint back to the Ala Wai's mouth. With light trades and a small swell, they made good time, particularly in the upwind legs.

Like most steersmen, Rigg didn't allow conversation in the boat, the exception being the leisurely cool-down coming back up the canal to the canoe ramp. As long as everybody made their changes and kept the easier pace, they could use their return leg to catch up on news and gossip, talk about families and jobs, and generally relax after the workout. Rigg himself chatted with Bear, who had provided his pickup truck and some heavy-lifting assistance for the recent move to Diamond Head.

"Thanks, man, I couldn't have done it without you," Rigg

said. "Especially getting the big stuff in through those doors."

"No problem, brother. You got a pickup, sooner or later everybody asks you to help with a move or take stuff to the dump, or whatever. How do you like the place?"

"It's fine. It feels wrong, though, a police officer living up there on the Gold Coast."

"Hey, you got the money, you can afford it."

"Kawika likes it. I guess I do, too."

Bear wanted to hear how the day had gone, the first day of real work in six months. "Must feel pretty strange, all that time at home, you gotta get back in the swing of things."

"It would, except they're not giving me anything to do, really. We'll see what happens."

"I thought maybe they'd give you something important to do. Homicide or narcotics."

"No, I think those days are over," Rigg said.

Off the boat ramp, Rigg leaned on the steering paddle, angling the flat blade so that the boat swung wide toward the shore, grounding gently on the bank. "Good workout, guys," he said. "Wednesday we're gonna go all the way down to the airport, turn around and push it home, so get a good night's sleep."

TEN

TO TOP OFF HIS DAY, Rigg and Kawika drove to his wife's condo in Makiki. "We'll celebrate your going back to work," Sandy had said. They weren't divorced and they weren't exactly married; their relationship in a something of an emotional twilight zone. Both of them hoped they could patch up a relationship frayed by job stresses and other issues, then shredded by the strains of Rigg's lawsuit. Sandy's relationship with another attorney in her office hadn't helped, nor had Iwalani Hu. Kawika divided his time between the two houses, and Rigg's move to Stone's cottage was the first step in reestablishing a single home.

Sandy's job as a Deputy Prosecuting Attorney had let Rigg stay in touch with goings-on in the law enforcement community during his long exile, and Sandy's condo had been the place where the whole whistle-blower thing had started. He'd been over for dinner one night, the two of them separated but talking vaguely about putting their relationship into rehab, mostly dancing around the big issues. She'd asked him to take Kawika for a couple of weeks, saying she had a big trial coming up.

"It should last at least two weeks, and I'll be working late every night," she said.

"No problem," he answered. "Who's the crook?"

"Gill Yoshino. He used to be a lawyer till his license got suspended. Narco raided his house and got an ounce of crystal meth."

"I think I heard about it."

"Probably from Andy Gomes. He used to be your partner, didn't he?"

"Gomes? No, he worked for me when he was a patrolman, but he wouldn't talk to me. He hates my guts."

"Really? Why is that?"

"Because the dumbass left a surveillance to go see his girlfriend, then wrote up the log like he'd never gone. He would've got away with it, except the crook he was supposed to be watching went to meet with one of our informants, and he calls me up, all in a panic. I wrote Gomes up and he got suspended. He hasn't forgotten about it."

Sandy came out from behind the counter, a steaming pot of rice in one hand and a stunned look on her face. "That can't be right," she said. "That's not possible."

Rigg laughed. "Sure it is. I was there at the hearing. He got 10 days on the beach for that little stunt. If anything had happened to the informant I'd have recommended him for prosecution, I was so pissed off."

"But the department told us … They certified him, told us no disciplinary actions."

"Somebody blew it, then. It's in his file, this only happened like four or five years ago."

Sandy put the rice on the counter. "But I represented to the court that we had made the search and hadn't found anything."

"Did you look at his file yourself?"

"No. Somebody from HPD does it. They tell us, and we tell the court."

"Don't worry about it, then. Somebody missed it. Probably some clerk in personnel. Go in tomorrow and ask 'em to take another look."

"You don't understand. We were supposed to do all that disclosure months ago. I'm going to trial on Monday morning."

"It can't be the end of the world."

Sandy sat down heavily on one of the dining room chairs. "It might be. The case law, starting with Henthorn in the federal courts, says the defense has the right to look at any adverse personnel action that's based on 'moral turpitude.' If somebody falsifies a report and gets disciplined for it, that whole record has to be given over in discovery to the defense so they can cross-examine the officer about it. You can imagine how that sounds to the jury. 'Oh, you lied in this report but not in the one involving my client?' If the officer is a key witness it's almost fatal for the prosecution. Mike Stone's representing Yoshino. He's not going to stop with ripping Gomes to shreds, Kimo. He's going to ask the court to sanction me."

"What? How are you supposed to know? You relied on somebody at HPD. How is it your fault?"

"I'm the officer of the court, not somebody from HPD. I'm the one who told the judge we didn't find anything. He's going to hold me accountable. He'll start by throwing out the case, probably, although my boss will most likely tell us to move for dismissal first."

"That doesn't seem right."

"How could this get overlooked? Do you think it was just a mistake?"

Rigg thought about it. "It's not really likely. The paper-work for a suspension is pretty extensive, what with the union getting involved, hearings and all that stuff. It would be hard to miss, and besides, most of the department knew about Gomes' deal." He shook his head. "No, it sounds like you got sandbagged."

Sandy went to the wall phone in the kitchen. "I've got to call my boss. He might want to hear it from you, might have some questions."

"Okay," Rigg said. "But I've got a question."

Dialing the phone, Sandy said, "What?"

"Do you think this is the only time it's happened?"

"I've been asking myself the same thing," she said grimly.

It turned out that it wasn't the first time it had happened, or the 50th. Somebody at personnel had been instructed by somebody else, who'd been told by somebody else, not to report certain of those "adverse personnel actions" to the prosecutor. When this came out, everybody in Honolulu's criminal justice system except the defense attorneys got very angry.

Judges were mad because they never like being lied to, and especially not by the government, but also because they're not used to having their orders ignored. The Honolulu Prosecuting Attorney was pissed because his people had been cruising confidently down to the courthouse every day and making all sorts of representations that turned out to be utterly false. The deputy prosecutors were cranky with anybody from HPD because the judges were mad and taking it out on the prosecutors in court. And the HPD brass was really annoyed with whoever had tipped off the judges and the lawyers to their little indiscretion. Being an investigative agency, they figured out who this person was fairly quickly.

Almost any bureaucracy will, when confronted with a bad situation of its own manufacture, take the time-honored route made famous by Richard Nixon and his Watergate bandits. They cover up. Edmund Chin did the covering for HPD, and he started by making a determined effort to get rid of the source of the trouble. Ian Rigg found himself on the receiving end of a cyclone of abuse. He tried pretending that the storm would blow itself out, but got tired quickly of going to work feeling like he was in somebody's crosshairs all the time. He made a list of all of the disciplinary actions he could remember that fit Sandy's "moral turpitude" meter, passing them to her one day at the condo. Her boss started talking about prosecuting police officials and the brass started talking about firing Rigg.

Mike Stone had been more than happy to take Rigg on as a client and to file the whistle-blower lawsuit. He hadn't been so pleased when Rigg told him to leave the City and County of Honolulu off the defendant's list.

"I don't want to take money from the taxpayers. Why should they have to pay because Chin's a moron?" Rigg told him.

"But that's the deep pocket," Stone had said, "the pot of gold."

"I'll settle for the pot of brass then," Rigg told him. "And I want my job back."

That proved to be a good call, though. The City's lawyers, overjoyed at not having to defend the taxpayers, abandoned Chin and the other two ranking officers, who had to find their own counsel. Chin had professional malpractice insurance, which covered most of his legal bills and would end up paying the judgment. HPD also backed the three straight down the line, offering up excuses for their conduct and ruling in a departmental hearing that they'd done no wrong in the exercise of their official judgment. One captain did get demoted for, as Stone put it sarcastically, "some other, completely unrelated, totally unconnected bit of malfeasance," and another retired early. It took nine months, but Rigg returned, with back pay and $1 million in Kawika's college fund.

The initial judgment had been for $2.5 million, actual and punitive damages, plus attorney's fees, but Chin's insurance company offered to settle for a lot less and Rigg agreed, provided he stayed a detective and there would be no more retaliation. The judge, approving the settlement, made a strong statement against Rigg's principal tormentor, and said if he heard about any future problems, he would hammer Chin into the ground like a tent peg. There were quite a few "never in all my days," "I never believed," and "this is a dark day for law enforcement" parts in the judge's speech, and most people thought Edmund Chin had gotten the message.

Now a year later, at Sandy's condo, with Kawika doing homework in the bedroom and the two of them sharing a bottle of white zinfandel on the lanai, she voiced the same opinion, telling Rigg she thought he'd have clear sailing because "nobody, not even Chin, is that stupid."

Rigg knew better, knew that Edmund Chin would keep pushing until something gave. He told her so, saying you'd never get rich betting on how smart that guy is, and he thought more trials were ahead. That was when he recited for the first time the newly minted motto of the Special Unsolved Crimes Section. "It sucks, but what can you do?"

Eleven

Deputy Chief Edmund Chin saw the Scandinavian truck delivering the furniture in the basement parking lot, and it reminded him of places he wanted to go. It looked like a very nice desk, and he thought he might put in for another, slightly larger model, possibly made of koa wood. In the office across the hall from his, the Chief's desk, made of Hawaiian koa wood by prison inmates late in the 19th century, had once belonged—or so legend had it—to Honolulu's sheriff, the legendary surfer, swimmer, Olympian and waterman, Duke Kahanamoku.

Deputy Chiefs and below got something much less distinguished. Chin, who very much wanted to sit behind Duke's desk in the future, knew that the path to that office had gotten much rockier with the judge's ruling against him. He'd lost that battle, but by destroying Rigg, he could still win the war, proving to the Police Commission and anyone else watching that he'd been right about the "rogue detective" all along. Since the current Chief wasn't expected to leave for several years, and Rigg wasn't going anywhere for eight, Chin figured he had time to sort the whole mess out.

In the basement, the secret underground lair of Detective Ian Rigg was looking up. New furniture on a tasteful blue rug that exactly fit the former storeroom's floor made the place much homier. A floor lamp next to Rigg's new recliner and another lamp on the desk replaced the cold fluorescent lights. He brought in some silk plants and a couple of original watercolors of old Honolulu, along with Nate Silafau's fruit bat on a plaque. He left room for the boxes he expected, but he could now relax in relative comfort while he waited for the assignments to filter down from Major Hata upstairs.

The boxes showed up on Wednesday, delivered by two people from Records who told him how much they liked the office. Rigg had them stack the boxes six feet high directly in front of the door. Anyone accidentally looking in now would see a solid wall of cardboard. You had to walk all the way around the stack to see the new décor, but he didn't think he'd be having too many visitors. He opened the box containing the administrative files, dust and mildew and old memories floating toward him in the room's quiet.

There weren't a lot of happy times to remember in the Double-crosser case. The community, from the politicians on down, put enormous pressure on the task force to solve the crimes. Each new body meant another very visible, almost personal failure, and the strain told on the detectives and their bosses. Some relationships fractured, never to be repaired. After the fifth killing, the lieutenant in command had been abruptly transferred to Patrol, a new man brought in to "crack the whip." At least one task force detective had asked to be relieved and reassigned.

HPD had never had a serial murderer to catch before, and after they found the third victim at a local beach park, task force detectives flew off to Los Angeles, Seattle, Chicago and New York, all of which had sad experiences of their own to share. The media, demanding new information daily, began to get in the way, forcing the department to appoint a spokesperson and nail down leaks. The fear that someone would say something, even inadvertently, that would enable the killer to escape justice, or worse, to kill again, only added to the strain on everyone.

Leafing through the old reports, Rigg came upon names he hadn't heard for years. Some were officers now retired.

Others were haole girls with brown hair who would never get a day older than the one the Double-crosser ended. He looked at the old pictures, smiling teenagers in yearbook photos, some mug shots, some crime scene photographs, marble bodies under harsh lights. Amber Wheatley from a Christmas picture with her family. Amber with her throat slashed and her arms crossed over her head. He found the files for each individual victim, rooting through the boxes until he had one good picture of each girl, laying these all out on his new desk in the order that they died.

Carol Collins, 19, unemployed mother of a one-year-old boy. Found at the edge of Kaneohe Bay.

Amber Wheatley, 20, student and part-time waitress. Lived in Kailua, but found on the shore of Keehi Lagoon by the airport. They thought the Good Samaritan might have suggested that she wait out of the rain in his van while he changed her tire. Since nobody knew about the dangers lurking in white vans at the time, she probably did it.

Nancy Kerr, 17, high school student. They thought she had been taken while hitchhiking from a bus stop near Hanauma Bay. After she was found next to a dumpster in a little beach park between Diamond Head and Hawaii Kai, the number of women hitchhiking on Oahu dropped to near zero.

Cindy Diehl, 18, unemployed, but probably working as a prostitute in Waikiki. Vice picked Cindy up a month before she was ripped, after Amber but before Nancy, and warned her about strange men. "All I ever see is strange men," Cindy told them. She was dumped in Ala Moana Beach Park, one of Honolulu's busiest, and found the next morning by a female jogger, who threw up all over the crime scene.

Lindsay Cassel, 19, also believed to be a prostitute, based on field contact reports filed by Waikiki patrol officers.

After Lindsay was taken, HPD put out decoys in Waikiki and downtown, hoping to lure in the killer, nervous young police officers who fit the victim profile and who were now looking for a white male in his late 20s or early 30s, who dressed well, seemed fairly self-assured and was also very good with a knife. The decoys came up with nothing, and the Double-crosser passed on prostitutes for four months.

Leilani Green, 16, high school student, did not come home from school. Her worried mother went looking, turning out most of their Kailua neighborhood, but Leilani wasn't found until two days later, in Pearl Harbor. The killer must have put her down at low tide or dropped her in a stream, because she floated off into the harbor, where a Navy boat crew recovered her. By now, the task force could recognize one of their customers at a glance, and Leilani, whose picture showed a shy girl with braces, fit the profile perfectly.

Karen Scott, 20, a college student, disappeared from her apartment in Waikiki. The building cameras showed her going out in exercise attire, and she frequently jogged on the path around the Ala Wai Canal. Police searchers actually found a spot on the path where Karen might have been taken, the key to her apartment on a bungee cord lying in the bushes near an area where a van could have been parked close to the path. HPD took all their decoys out of Waikiki and started having them jog around town. Scott's body, laid out like all the others, was found by a man walking his dog next to the Hilton Hawaiian Village lagoon. A security camera at one of the nearby hotels recorded a white van on the street during the night, but the same tape also showed one or two hundred other cars and trucks.

Elaine Thomas, 20, was definitely a prostitute, with two prior arrests for soliciting. She was reported missing by her pimp, Otis Sampson, who told the responding detectives that losing Elaine "is gonna cost me $800 a night. I oughta sue y'all, 'cause if you mothers had been doing your fuckin' jobs, this never would've happened." One detective had to forcibly restrain the other from attacking Sampson. A patrolman looking for Elaine's body found her by the side of Kamehameha Highway on the North Shore. The killer had cut her to pieces, by far the most damage to any of the eight victims.

Rigg rummaged around and found two more pictures, those of Ray Streck and Stella Roddick, placing these next to the others. Streck fit the other profile, that of the man they so avidly hunted—not perfectly perhaps, but close. When the search of his van turned up a pair of handcuffs, human blood and Polaroid pictures of Elaine Thomas, naked and suffering, the task force thought they had their man. DNA testing would eventually link blood in the van to Collins and Thomas, victims one and eight, but none of the other six victims. The crime scene technicians said the interior of the vehicle could have been bleached in the past, which might have eliminated evidence of other crimes.

Ray Streck looked awfully good for the murders. In addition to the evidence found in his car and his house, a cigarette butt with Streck's DNA was found on Carol Collins, the first victim, along with some fibers that matched the van's cloth seats, and a few of his hairs, too. Being dead, he wasn't there to defend himself, but the investigation found nothing to suggest he hadn't done the crimes, which coincidentally stopped as soon as Streck died. With the other evidence from the house, the bosses were ready to declare their nightmare over. After flying to L.A. to interview Streck's ex-wife, Rigg left the task force, sent back to Narco to finish that tour. He left with questions he never thought would be answered, and one of the biggest was why had Streck picked the Double-cross trademark, and what had he been saying to them?

He pulled out the thick file on Streck from the box marked with his name. Detectives had gone over his life with a microscope, looking for the cues the FBI said would be there, the things that made you confident you were dealing with a serial killer. He started at the beginning, reading the summaries of witness statements, a psychological assessment, and a list of the items found in his townhouse. Three hours later, he left it all on his desk to go to paddling practice, the girls' pictures neatly lined up, their smiles haunting him again after four years of trying to forget.

Twelve

ON THURSDAY MORNING, several days ahead of schedule, the file on the unknown tagger who called himself "OZ MAN 1" arrived in his box at CID. The file came as a bit of a shock for Rigg, and not just because Major Hata had sent it down early. For one thing, the accordion folder bulged out to its full four inches. For another, it was lavishly illustrated, something you don't see that often in police reports.

And judging from the pictures, OZ MAN 1 had been a very busy boy, which provided the biggest surprise. The City and County Department of Transportation Services alone estimated OZ MAN 1's damages at $125,000. When you tacked on the damage to state signs, guardrails and other assets, and to the various pieces of private property he painted regularly, well, the total got grander every night.

"You can't believe this guy," Rigg told Silafau at lunch, the two of them meeting at Ono's, a Hawaiian hole-in-the-wall on Kapahulu. "He's tagged more than 300 places around the island. Sometimes five or six times. At one point, he had something on every freeway sign from Kahala to downtown. Even the little ones."

"That's a hardworking vandal," Silafau said.

"Yeah, and those signs are expensive as hell to replace, 15 or 20 grand a pop. I had no idea."

"Maybe it's more than one person. Did you think of that? There's supposed to be whole tagging crews out there," Silafau said.

"It's possible, but the gang intelligence people think he's a loner and probably a kid, maybe 15 or 16 years old. And catch this: he's got his own personal web site where he puts up pictures of his latest and greatest."

"Everybody's got a web site nowadays, even crooks," Silafau said. "How come you can't just nail him through that?"

"It's some kind of anonymous server, I don't get it, but even if you knew who was posting to it, you couldn't prove who did the actual painting. There's quite a few sites apparently that're devoted to tagging and graffiti art."

"So, you gonna take this thing serious or just play Chin's game?"

"Oh, I'm definitely gonna try and catch this guy. I wasn't going to at first. I figured, Criminal Property Damage, even first degree, why waste the prosecutor's time? The tagger wouldn't get any jail time, and you know my rule about that."

"Yep, that would be, 'Never work longer on a case than the crook's likely to spend in jail.' That rules out all of your misdemeanors, practically."

"Hell, you'd have to be a five-time loser before a state judge would give you any jail time for tagging, and OZ MAN 1's never been busted before, as far as anybody knows."

"So, why are you breaking your rule for this mope?"

"First of all, because I'd like to walk into Special Ed's office with the little punk in handcuffs, tell him I just solved his unsolved crime for him. But mostly because unless this kid's like 10, he's old enough to know better, and he makes the whole city look bad. I mean, we've got a beautiful town, and his so-called 'art' isn't making it any nicer. Makes the place look like Miami or South Central L.A., and nobody comes to Hawaii to see that crap." Rigg waved at the waitress for the check. "Nah, he broke one of my other rules, the one that goes, 'don't piss off the nice police officer,' and I'd like to see him pay for it."

Full of kalua pork and lau lau, they walked outside onto

busy Kapahulu Avenue, the Waikiki-bound cars whizzing past. Rigg pointed to the bank across the street. "That's one of his walls right there. His stuff's the red and black on the far end."

OZ MAN 1 signed his pieces, which made it easy to identify his work. Leafing through the photographs later, Rigg started to get an appreciation for the kid's talent and for the perverse conceit he took in keeping his art out front and in the public eye. Several times, he came across police reports from the same complainant, dated only a day or two apart. OZ MAN 1 had tagged a wall, the crime was reported to the police and the wall re-painted, and then he returned the next night to tag it again. It was apparently a point of pride that his work was never covered over for long.

Also rather amazing was the agility displayed in getting to some out-of-the-way spot or out on the support beam of a highway sign. This clown must be part mountain goat or tree squirrel, Rigg thought, looking at the pictures taken from ground level at graffiti 30 feet in the air.

None of the papers in the file gave any real clue as to OZ MAN 1's identity, though.

"The little bastard probably lives in town, because he checks on his work in the daytime, and it's pretty concentrated in one area," Rigg told Silafau. "I think if I stake out something he did the night before, he'd come by to check it or take a picture."

"Or you can hang out at a spot all night."

"There's an awful lot of places, but it may come to that."

Rigg checked on the paints, visiting a few auto supply and home improvement stores to see who'd been buying spray paint. If OZ MAN 1 was under 18, though, somebody else would be buying it for him. Nothing turned up. He talked to Bear, who found him four taggers who had been convicted and were now spending their weekends doing community service by painting over graffiti. He met them at Probation.

"That dude is radical," one said. "Tag king," said another. "He's everywhere," said a third. "I've painted over a bunch of his stuff," said the last. "It's awesome."

"Yeah, but who is he?"

"Who knows, man? The dude's super low key."

"Low key?" Rigg said. "What are you talking about? This is the least low key crook I ever went after. He's got his name more places in public than Madonna and Bill Clinton put together."

The taggers looked at each other, then at him. "Who's Bill Clinton?" one said.

He stayed out until midnight on Saturday night, sitting in a driveway down the street from a City and County fire station that OZ MAN 1 had visited. The tagger didn't come back. And if he hadn't been depressed enough, Sandy told him the Prosecuting Attorney wouldn't even try to charge OZ MAN 1 with all of the other damage he'd done.

"How can we prove that he did all the others? He'll say he just decided to imitate the real OZ MAN 1, and you caught him on his first night out. Whatever that damage is, that's what he'll have to eat. Unless he confesses, he's home free."

"Then I'll get him to confess."

"Good luck. Especially if he's a juvenile. You'll have a hard time even interviewing him without his parents there."

"Jeez, this is depressing," Rigg said.

"What is it you've been saying lately?" Sandy said. "'It sucks, but what can you do?'"

Thirteen

"Hey, buddy. What're you doing?" Rigg stood in the doorway of Kawika's room, that Friday night, taking in the collection of parts on the floor.

"Just cleaning up for tomorrow." Kawika was running a cotton patch down a two-foot length of blue pipe.

"Is that all your paintball gear?"

"Not all of it. I've got the face mask and stuff in the bag."

"This paintball thing's really taken off. I see the signs up here and there. You go over to Bellows, don't you?"

"Yeah, the Air Force Base, or down to Keehi Lagoon. There's a couple of places that are set up for battles on the weekend."

Rigg picked up a clear plastic hopper that usually fit on top of the paintball gun. "This feeds the balls into the gun, right?"

"We're supposed to call them 'markers,' not guns. And you 'mark' somebody; you don't 'shoot' them."

"Uh huh. Well, I expect you probably feel like you got shot, you get hit with one of those balls. How fast are they going?"

"Two-eighty or 300 feet per second. There's a chronograph at the tournament that measures the speed, and if you're higher than 300, you've got to lower the air pressure." Kawika started assembling the parts.

"I'll bet that stings."

"It depends on where you get hit. Sometimes you can't even feel it. On your hand hurts a lot, or in the neck. If you're not wearing a cup and you get shot there, that really hurts."

"I thought you weren't getting shot."

"Marked, then. Everybody gets marked. There's so many paintballs flying around, it's hard not to."

"How fast does this thing shoot?" Rigg picked up the assembled marker, an ungainly contraption of steel and aluminum, with a bottle of compressed air where the stock would be.

"If you're on full auto with this magazine," Kawika reached over and attached the hopper to the gun, "thirty rounds a second."

"Holy cow."

"You want to hear?" Kawika flipped a switch on the grip and pointed the gun at his pillow. A sharp ripping sound filled the room, the gun coughing 30 blasts of compressed air in almost a single explosion.

"And your pastor's fine with all of this, huh?"

"He's played a couple of times, but the youth pastor takes us. We've got almost everybody in the junior high Sunday school classes in our group."

"It's the church group tomorrow at Bellows?"

"Yeah. The school paintball club is next week at Keehi." Kawika put a plug in the barrel, unscrewing the compressed air tank and flipping open a black nylon case. Inside were tubes filled with silver-colored paintballs, and what looked to Rigg like a pair of hand grenades.

"What do you use those for?" he said.

"The grenades? When somebody's in a bunker you can throw one of these."

"Does it work?"

"Yeah, but they're like, $7 dollars each, so you've got to save them for when you really need them."

"And they've got the same paint in them, too?"

"Yeah. It all washes off. It's biodegradable. All the paintballs are made out of the stuff they use to make Tylenol capsules or something like that, so when it rains, they dissolve."

"Amazing. It sounds like a blast."

"It's a lot of fun. You can rent a marker at Bellows. All you need then is the air and the paint and a mask. They've got all that stuff there."

"Who are you guys going up against tomorrow?"

"All kinds of people. There's usually a lot of Marines over there, and army guys. I've seen people from your work there. Probably other church groups, and just the hard-core ones that come out there early and don't go home till after dark. You should go. You don't work on Saturday, do you?"

"Not yet. Not tomorrow. I'm not part of your group, though."

"It doesn't matter. They'll put you on a team that needs extra people. It would be fun."

And that was how Ian Rigg ended up spending part of his weekend at a beach in Waimanalo, getting blasted from three sides by church youth group kids who stalked him with a relentless fanaticism he was fairly sure they hadn't learned in Sunday school. At least he hoped not. He spent much of the afternoon examining his welts in the dead box, watching the kids go at each other. This gave him quite a bit of free time to think about Stella Roddick and the eight others killed years before. He knew who had killed the eight, or thought he did. But who had killed Stella, and why?

Fourteen

Rigg saw the Camry for the second time on Monday when he stopped at Nguyen Nguyen's Bistro Italiano. He ate at the Bistro regularly, but he also went to see Nguyen, a long-time informant with great contacts in Honolulu's Southeast Asian community. The Camry stopped about a block short of the restaurant on King Street. Nobody got out. Rigg thought about the possibilities over linguine and clam sauce, Silafau chatting up one of the waitresses in Thai, his other language.

"Ain't it great?" Silafau said. "Hawaii's got to be the only place in the world where a half-Samoan, half-Frenchman can get Italian food fixed by a Vietnamese chef and served by a Thai waitress."

"Yeah, do me a favor, will you, Nate?" Rigg said as they got ready to go. "Hang around here for a minute or two and see if anybody takes off after me."

"Sure. You think it's Special Ed, coming back for more?"

"I don't know. He's the likeliest suspect, and the dumbest."

"What am I looking for?"

"I saw a green Camry. Call me on my cell if you get a plate number."

Rigg didn't need Silafau to catch the Ford Explorer pulling out of a parallel spot half a block down. When he got the call, the Explorer had dropped off and the Camry was back.

"You were right. The white Ford SUV, and I think he's working with a green Toyota like you said," Silafau said.

"Did you get the plates?"

Silafau had, and Rigg asked him to run them at DEA and give him a call. He was going to stay on the road until he had everybody behind him sorted into their proper places.

"I'll come by the federal building in half an hour, go once around the block like I'm looking for a parking place. Maybe you can watch from the sidewalk and see if I've missed anybody," Rigg said.

This ploy picked up two more cars. All four were registered to the same leasing company.

"Never mind that," Silafau said. "I know one of those guys driving, worked with him on a case about six months ago. He was assigned to CIU. I think the leasing place is one of their fronts."

HPD's secretive Criminal Intelligence Unit reports directly to the Chief of Police and works under cover on the most sensitive assignments in the department. Rigg had done a couple of years in CIU, leaving because they never actually put anybody in jail, only gathered information for others. They collected much of this intelligence by pulling surveillance, giving them more practice than anybody else in the department and making CIU very good. He'd been lucky to spot the tail. And if CIU was on him, he had big problems.

"They've got a four-car surveillance on me," Rigg said. "Six people. That's a lot of manpower."

"Especially if they're going around the clock," Silafau said. "We can't even do that for long on big-time dope dealers. You must've really pissed somebody off."

"People keep telling me that. Man, I don't know. I wasn't expecting this stuff to start up so quick."

Rigg thought about confronting his followers, maybe trying to find out who'd set them on him and why, but he suspected they might not even know themselves. More probably, they'd been given the assignment and were just following orders. He pulled over into an open metered parking spot, opened the OZ MAN 1 file and got the address of a bank near the University of Hawaii that had been tagged only a week before. "Might as well start someplace," he said, checking traffic and pulling back out. Behind him, the green Camry and the white Ford fell into line.

Central Hawaiian Bank's University branch had a nice curving white wall that faced a movie theater on busy University Avenue. OZ MAN 1 had delivered his judgment on both wall and bank one night a few days before Rigg got the file, leaving an intricate, multi-color spray paint challenge of words and symbols. It was definitely an OZ MAN 1 creation; the tagger's signature was repeated at least 20 times in the mural.

Following OZ MAN 1's first strike, the bank reported the crime to the police and repainted the wall. Rigg saw that the tagger had returned, hitting again on the fresh coat of white paint. He thought the latest creation didn't have the same style and character as the first. The statement here was not at all cryptic. OZ MAN 1 couldn't be stopped.

We'll see about that, Rigg thought, and went inside the bank to look for the manager, planning to ask when the latest tagging had taken place. This was when the big graffiti investigation got sidetracked for an hour and a half.

The man at teller window number 3 immediately drew Rigg's attention. Wearing an army fatigue jacket and a Yankees baseball hat, he looked more than a little out of place, especially since all Hawaii banks prohibited any kind of headwear and didn't like sunglasses, either. He had a paper sack on the counter in front of him, and Rigg caught a glimpse of cash going into the bag. He also noted the terrified expression on the teller's face.

Turning on his heel, Rigg left the bank through the front

door, checking first to see if anyone seemed to be waiting outside, then standing on the sidewalk and watching through the glass as the baseball cap finished his transaction. Paper sack in hand, the Yankees fan turned for the door, coming toward Rigg but keeping his head down, hiding his face beneath the bill of the cap. He stopped in the doorway, stuffing the paper sack down into his jeans, then pushed open the door.

"Police," Rigg said when the man came out onto the sidewalk. "Get on the ground, face first." Rigg had his gun out and in the man's face. The Yankees fan looked around, maybe thinking about running.

"Don't. Don't even think about it. Keep your hands where I can see them, and get on the ground. Now."

"I didn't do nothin', man," the Yankees fan said, but he lowered himself to the ground, face down.

"Uh huh. We're gonna see about that. But first I want you to take that bag out of your pants. Roll over on your back. Keep your right hand out to your side, then reach in with your left hand, pull the bag out real slow and toss it over there by the door. If you come out with anything but paper, I'm gonna cap your ass, so let's get this right."

"I got nothin' in my pants."

"No? That's what you say, and if you don't move pretty quick, you're gonna be right about that."

"There's nothing there," the Yankees fan said, sounding a little whiny.

"Don't argue with me, shitbird. Do what I tell you or you're gonna be real sorry."

"I don't know what you're talking about," the Yankees fan said, but he thought about it for a couple of seconds, then rolled over as instructed, reaching for his waistline. He fumbled around in his pants and had just got the bag out of the jeans when it exploded with a dull pop, flinging red dye, a cloud of smoke, and a fine spray of tear gas all over the robber, the sidewalk, and the bank's front door. Money, released from the bag, fluttered down onto the pavement, blowing toward the street.

"That's what I'm talking about," Rigg said. "Man, it's a good thing you know how to listen, otherwise you'd never be making any little baby bank robbers. Now, roll back over and put your hands on your head."

The Yankees fan, choking and crying from the gas, moved a little faster this time, the sound of sirens in the distance. Rigg eased upwind out of the man's line of sight and into a position where he could be seen clearly from the street. He hoped the CIU people on the surveillance would let the responding patrol officers know he was there and one of the good guys.

An hour and a half later, Rigg got back in the Porsche. He'd given statements to the robbery detectives and the FBI agents who showed up, talked for a minute to the teller who'd been robbed, and chatted for a few more with the robber, now a fine shade of red, who wanted to thank him for getting the explosives out of his shorts before they went off. "No problem," Rigg told him. "Remember, Mr. Police Officer is your friend."

He noticed the little splotches of red dye on his arms, trousers, and shirt in the bank, asking the branch manager how long it took to wear off.

"That's good stuff," the manager said. "It won't wash off, but it'll wear off in a week or so."

"Swell," Rigg said.

"And your clothes are ruined. It won't come out of fabric at all. Sorry. But we appreciate your catching the man. It was lucky you were here."

"That reminds me," Rigg said. "I wanted to talk to you about that graffiti outside. Just got distracted with all the fuss."

And he did a short interview to get his case back on track.

His message light blinked at him when he got back to the cave to write up the report on the bank robbery arrest. Cal Kamaka wanted a call, but Rigg decided to go upstairs, deliver the report in person. While he was at it, he'd see if he could get any vibes from the staff in CID. He remembered all too well the feeling of isolation before, when friends avoided him and the polite excusal became a standard feature in his life. When he got upstairs he did pick up some negative energy but allowed that paranoia could easily be setting in.

The feeling came back, though, when he found Kamaka, who glanced around the room twice when Rigg walked up, looking exactly like somebody afraid to be seen talking to somebody else.

"What's up, Cal?" Rigg said.

"I was following up on your statement from Monday," Kamaka said, putting it in the middle of his desk. "I just needed to ask you a couple more questions."

"Shoot," Rigg said.

"Well, you start with the car, but what were you doing before that?"

"What do you mean?"

"Like, where were you before you saw the car?"

"That's in there," Rigg said, gesturing at the report. "I was up in the driveway, warming up, then I started the run about 4:30."

"No. I've got that. I mean before you started, where were you?"

"Sleeping. What else would I be doing?"

"It looks pretty bad, Kimo," Kamaka said.

"What are you talking about? What looks bad?"

"All of it. You knew Stella Roddick, she gets dumped right next to your house. The same day, you go to the major and get the original file on her and take it all with you someplace."

"Yeah, but you know why I did that. That can't be everything."

"No. The rest of it is, with Streck dead, who else knew about the Double-crosser's M.O.? Who knew about the cuts on the victims' feet?"

Now Rigg got it, didn't want to believe, but saw clearly where everything had led. "What the hell? They think I killed Stella?"

Kamaka looked away. "I don't think they really think that. I know I don't, but you know Chin. He'd love to get you on something and Martin would be happy to help. So, I gotta ask you. Where were you Monday morning about three o'clock? Because that's when the M.E. thinks Stella died."

"They think I killed Stella," Rigg said. It wasn't a question anymore. It was a statement, now. "Holy shit."

PART
II

Fifteen

Monday

Being hunted wasn't exactly a new experience for Rigg. He'd been there before in the run-up to the lawsuit, with Internal Affairs sniffing around for something to hang on him and everyone in the department choosing up sides or sitting on the fence. He busied himself in the office with the Double-crosser files that afternoon, but driving toward paddling practice he watched the mirror constantly, hating the suspicions, the old saying that even a paranoid can have real enemies playing in his head.

He didn't want to be alone with those old sayings or the paranoid feelings, and he arranged to meet his lawyer at Nguyen's after practice. Predictably, Mike Stone hit the roof.

"This is total bullshit. You're not even back there a week and they're hanging all over you like this morning's wash. I can't believe it. This is worse than retaliation. It could even be criminal harassment."

"Calm down," Rigg told him. "They're investigating a murder, and they're right. People who know the Double-crosser's M.O. would be suspects in this case." That presumably meant everyone who had been on the task force, himself included.

"Right," Stone said, the sarcasm dripping. "I'm sure they've got CIU following everybody who worked that case. Or is it just you?"

"I'm the logical one," Rigg said. "They find the body practically on my doorstep. They've got to check it out."

"So why don't they just ask? You've got an alibi. Kawika was there at the house."

"Kawika was in bed by 10. That was a school night, and those are the rules. He slept through all the commotion down below when they found Roddick. I had to wake him up when I came back. Could I have gone out after 10, driven to where she was living, snatched her and brought her back before 4:30? It's not that far and that's six and a half hours, so yeah, I could. The time thing works."

"What's the motive, then? Why the hell would you kill anybody, much less somebody who was a witness from an old case?"

"Yeah, that's where it starts to get shaky. But they're gonna come up with something, you can bet on that. These are some motivated mothers. You can see how good this would sound for them. If I get busted for murder, Chin would've been right about me all along. Everybody would forget about the bad stuff he did, this would be so freakin' sensational."

"They'll never get a jury to buy it. There's so much reasonable doubt, a first-year law student could win this case."

Rigg shook his head. "You've got to be joking. Even if I got acquitted in the end, everybody in town would think I just had a sharp lawyer and beat the same system I beat once before for a million bucks. But I'm a murderer in everybody's mind, and there's no way I'm getting my job back after that deal, either."

Stone started to object, then conceded the point. "Yeah, we can't let it get that far," he said.

"I don't know if we can stop it. They'll be itching to collar somebody for this thing, and I'm the hottest suspect. Think about it. Whoever killed Roddick knew something that only about 10 people on the whole planet are supposed to know. At least one of those people, Ray Streck, is definitely dead. I don't know where the rest of them are, but it's a safe bet that some of them are covered for Monday morning. They retired to another island, they're in Vegas for the weekend. In bed with their wives. Whatever. And none of them were living upstairs from where the body was dumped. It's narrowing down pretty fast."

"Okay, but we come back to motive. Why would you do this? It doesn't make any sense at all."

"It might," Rigg said. "I've been thinking a lot about it since this afternoon." Actually, he'd thought about nothing else on the long paddle out and back past Waikiki, coming up with a host of troubling possibilities. "How about this one? What if Stella and I got involved during the original case, maybe we cooked up something for the reward. Cops get too close to witnesses and informants sometimes. Maybe I wanted to shut her up, but I have to wait until I'm back on the force so I can keep track of the investigation. And I'm a witness; I tell them I see a white van, send them off in the wrong direction."

Stone looked skeptical, and Rigg gave him the point. "Okay, that's a long shot, but if I thought of it, they will, and all they've got to do is go back through the files and see if they can't find some facts that fit their little picture. Only guess what? They don't have the old files. I do. How suspicious is that?"

"There's a reasonable explanation."

"Actually, there isn't. I've got no business asking for those files. Stella's homicide wasn't my case and the Double-crosser's been closed for years. Hata should've told me 'no.' He's probably in hot water now for doing it."

"Jesus, Kimo, you're starting to sound suspicious to me."

Rigg laughed. "And you can imagine how those guys are right now. Martin and Chin'll be drooling all over themselves, seeing something fishy in everything I've said or done for the last week."

Stone looked depressed, but Rigg hadn't finished yet. "And those CIU people on surveillance outside are gonna be reporting back tomorrow that I met with my lawyer right after I talked to Kamaka. That sounds guilty, too."

"There's no crime in that," Stone said, looking around like he wanted to tell the watchers the same thing. "You've got a Fourth Amendment right …"

"Hey, you don't have to tell me," Rigg said. "I'm just saying how it looks to somebody who already wants to nail me to the wall."

"Okay. You got anything else?"

"Yeah, but this one goes deep into Paranoia-ville. Let's say there's somebody who really, really doesn't like me. They need to discredit me, but whatever they try has to be so strong it'll get past this legal shield I've got. Murder would do it, for sure, and they set it all up. I'm not the only one in the department who knows the Double-crosser's M.O., but I'm the one who lives 20 yards away from the body dump. Then all they have to do is a regular murder investigation with me as the suspect, do a warrant, find something of Stella's or a weapon in my place, and I'm toast."

"You think somebody in the department killed this girl?" Stone, who had served as the police union's attorney in the past, sat back, aghast.

"No, actually, I don't. Chin hates me, no doubt. And he's a complete jerk, but I don't think he's a killer. And as much as the conspiracy kooks and nutcases out there would like to think so, government agencies and police departments just aren't suited for some big, complex, evil scheme. We're not devious enough and we're not built that way. Hell, we can barely keep the secrets we're supposed to have, much less the ones we're not."

Rigg nodded to the waitress who'd brought the dinner check. "Thanks. No, it's not likely, but it is possible. I hurt some people with the lawsuit. Messed up some careers. One guy, pissed off enough, he could do it. I can't rule it out, so I've got to keep it in play."

"What's our approach, then?" Stone asked.

"It all depends on how much time I've got before they close it out. If they jump too soon, they won't have the whole frame built. They'll know it'll collapse fast and won't get past the Deputy Prosecutor who does the screening. They don't want to wait too long, either, because if I'm really the target, they want to hit me as soon as they've got the ammo. Wouldn't want to delay that gratification."

Rigg saw the downcast expression on Stone's face, appreciated the concern. "Don't worry, it's not all bad news," he said.

"Oh, yeah? You got some good news, I'd love to hear it."

"Well, if there's another killer out there and he starts laying out young haole girls again, I'm gonna have a rock-solid alibi for those."

"What's that?"

Rigg snorted. "I've got six CIU people watching everything I do."

"But that means you think there could be another killer out there."

"No, I know for a fact there's another killer out there. I didn't do Stella, but somebody sure did. What I don't know is whether this is the first murder in a new string, or there's something else going on."

"What are you going to do?"

Rigg stood up. "Nothing much. I've just got to find the son of a bitch who killed Roddick before they do, *and* before Martin can talk the Prosecutor into filing for an arrest warrant for me. If I was them putting this together, I'd go for the warrant on Friday afternoon. That would let them hold me in jail till arraignment on Monday morning. That gives me three, three and a half days, tops."

"Where do you even start to do something like that?"

"I don't know. I've never had to do it before, solve a murder on my own. But I figure I'll start with the Double-crosser file, since it's in my office already."

But when the door to the cave opened on Tuesday morning, Rigg, ready to go to work, noticed the change right away. It was hard not to. Every box from the Double-crosser file was gone.

Sixteen

They'd left a receipt for all 32 boxes. Jerome Martin had signed it. Rigg saw that although they'd checked his desk for anything he'd taken out of the boxes, they'd courteously left him the OZ MAN 1 file. The cave had a roomier feel again.

Before he did anything else, Rigg completely rearranged the SUCS office. He moved all of the furniture, the computer equipment, and the phone to the very front of the room, into the place formerly occupied by stacks of boxes. Since everything was completely empty, it didn't take long, and when he was done, he got to work on the computer.

The week before and on the previous afternoon, Rigg had scanned almost two full boxes of Double-crosser records into his computer. This included all of the reports relating to Stella, all of the administrative reports, the daily logs, and the summaries of each homicide. He had lists of all the witnesses, all the exhibits, and some of the interviews. He also had an index of the entire file and a list of everyone who had worked on the case or been at a Double-crosser crime scene.

The Double-crosser had been one of the last major cases at HPD worked the old-fashioned way, with paper police reports. Now, everything was digitized in the department's mainframe computer, and if Ray Streck had lived, somebody would probably have gone back and scanned the old reports into the new system. Thinking he could use the computer to crunch some of the data for him, Rigg had started to create his own digital file on the case. Now he had a more urgent need for the information, which he hoped they'd left on his hard drive.

They had, and Rigg burned four CDs with the file, erasing it from his hard drive and putting the disks inside Foucault's book. They might be able to recreate his computer activity, even recover the file, but he had the working copies and they might not figure that out for a while. The clock now ticking, he got the OZ MAN 1 folder and headed for the door, picking up the book on the way out, resisting the urge to wave to the surveillance camera he was certain they'd installed the night before.

They were still keeping an eye on him outside, too. Taking off on King Street, Rigg rolled past Nguyen's Bistro, looking for his tail. He needed to verify that they were on him without being too obvious in his counter-surveillance measures, so he squared a block and performed a couple other moves that generally turn up a tail. CIU was using different cars today, but they were back there, and Rigg called up Stone to let him know he still had company. "They're on me," he told his lawyer on the cell phone. "It looks pretty loose. I don't think they're ready to move in yet."

"Well, at least you've still got that alibi you were talking about. Anything happens now, you're gonna be okay."

"Maybe. Keep your cell phone on," Rigg told him. "In case the next time I call you, it's from the payphone in the cellblock."

Rigg drove around for half an hour, taking it easy on his followers, trying to get his "Things to Do" list organized in the proper order. When he thought he had it down, he drove to Ala Moana Shopping Center, where he picked up a lightweight and pricey laptop computer. Adding on some bells and whistles, including wireless Internet service, a printer, a scanner and a GPS mapping program, set him back almost $4,000, but when he drove out onto Ala Moana Boulevard, he had a complete mobile office and a good-sized chunk of the Double-crosser file right there in his car.

By noon, he had pictures of half a dozen of OZ MAN 1's biggest and most extravagant creations on his new computer. He also interviewed the property owners and a couple of neighbors, trying to nail down an approximate time when the actual tagging took place. The best he could do was "nighttime," although he did establish that OZ MAN 1 struck not more than two days after the owners had painted over the last mess on their property. "It costs me 50 bucks, just in paint, every time I've got to clean up after that little bastard," the owner of one wall in Kaimuki said. "I'm tempted to wait out here one night with a baseball bat."

"You do that," Rigg told him, "and he'll sue your ass. He wins, he might wind up owning the wall."

The owner looked at the mural. "That's what my wife said. You better catch him. I'm starting to think it might be worth it."

Tuesday afternoon

They say you can't feel high blood pressure, but Rigg knew this was baloney. He'd felt it plenty over the past year, sometimes for weeks at a time. He had migraine headaches that lasted for days, and at one point, with the stress pounding at him, he'd developed a nasty case of shingles, spending a month with pain gnawing at his side like a hungry wolverine. He'd gone in to the Kaiser clinic, the doctor whistling at the lesions, asking him, "Are you under any stress right now? Because that could trigger it."

He also knew that the pain and the blood pressure got worse during the downtime, when he had nothing to do but think about the worst that could happen and worry about the future. The department had put him on administrative leave with pay, but all that did was stretch that down time into endless hours spent going over the evidence in his case, the pain eating at him. And nobody had been trying to pin a murder on him back then.

His appetite a distant memory, but knowing he needed to eat, Rigg stopped at a lunch wagon, picking up a plate lunch before driving down Kalanianaole Highway toward Hawaii Kai. With the familiar smell of beef stew and rice filling the Porsche, he stopped at the little beach park where they'd found Nancy Kerr four years earlier. He eased the plate onto his lap and looked at the spot where the Double-crosser left her, little waves splashing up onto the narrow strip of sand, bigger ones crashing onto the reef offshore.

That was the trouble with his job, he thought. Nobody saw Hawaii like a detective, and this was definitely his loss. After more than 20 years on the job, he associated virtually every place on the island with some crime or criminal. He'd done a search warrant down that street. He'd made a domestic violence arrest in that condo. A major ice dealer lived up on that ridge. In his undercover days, it seemed like he'd bought drugs in almost every beach park and public parking lot on the island. And this pretty little beach where tourists stopped to take pictures of the sunset? This would always and forever be a crime scene where some bastard ripped someone's daughter and left her out like this morning's trash. Memories like that made Honolulu a completely different place for Rigg and people like him.

He got out of the car and threw the beef stew into the dumpster, settling back in to organize his OZ MAN 1 file, sorting the pictures and trying to find some pattern in the vandal's operation. Nothing jumped out at him, as doubts muttered in the background.

"That's enough of that crap," he told the computer, finally. He checked on his surveillance, the Dodge Caravan still parked down at the far end of the parking area, then put one of the Double-crosser CDs in the drive, bringing up the files. He started in the logical place, with the woman whose body had been dumped less than 50 yards from his house. What had happened to her in the last four years? What had brought her to Diamond Head that morning, and was she victim number one of the new killer, or victim number nine of the old one?

The computer said that Stella Roddick had moved from her Kaneohe townhouse to Honolulu about a year before. She had a rental unit off Date Street, in an area of run-down older apartment buildings and new, high-rise condominiums. He thought he'd drive over and check it out, but for this trip, he didn't want any company.

Starting the Porsche, he moved out slowly, letting the surveillance get settled in behind him as he headed back towards town. When he thought they were comfortable, he jumped off the freeway and into one of the neighborhoods on the back side of Diamond Head, a warren of short blocks and blind corners. Speeding up, he made a turn at every intersection for about five minutes, dodging back and forth through the neighborhood, never going in a straight line for more than a few seconds. At one point, he passed one of the surveillance cars going in the opposite direction, seeing its brake lights flash in his rear view mirror as he disappeared around another corner.

When he was fairly certain he'd lost everyone, and was pretty confused about where he was himself, he took off in a beeline, the street empty behind him. Within 10 minutes, he was at Stella Roddick's new apartment. "What a freakin' dump," he said to the computer when he got there.

Stella had lived on the fourth floor in a one-bedroom unit that overlooked the Ala Wai Canal. You could almost see his canoe club's launching ramp from her front door, and if you leaned out over the railing, you could look down to the seaward end of Diamond Head. Rigg's new house was less than a mile and a half away. The narrow lanai in back faced the parking structure of another, much nicer condominium that soared 30 stories higher than Stella Roddick's last home.

The building manager, a pot-bellied California transplant, looked at Rigg's badge and said yeah, he still had a key to her place, and don't you need another warrant to get in there? Rigg told him the first one was still good, which wasn't technically true, but he thought maybe violating the constitutional rights of a dead lady was the least of his problems at the moment.

Roddick's apartment had been thoroughly and efficiently searched, and most of the smooth surfaces were covered with dustings of black, white or gray fingerprint powder. A copy of the search warrant, dated a week ago exactly, lay with a list of the items seized on the dining table, along with Jerome Martin's business card. Quite a few of the items were the kinds of thing homicide investigators routinely take from a crime scene: a piece of carpet, a hairbrush, pieces of clothing. Because murder victims are frequently killed by people they know, Martin had taken lots of papers with names, addresses and phone numbers, hoping like Rigg that the name of the killer was in there somewhere.

Rigg got a sense of where Martin was heading by looking at the things he'd seized. Something that might hold a blood-stain would tell him if Stella had been killed here. There weren't too many of these. Martin took things that could retain the killer's fingerprints or some DNA. Rigg counted about 10 of these. He also saw that the list ended with three interesting items: an address book, a color photograph and an HPD Miscellaneous Crime Report dated four years earlier. Rigg wrote down the report number and the date.

He stood for a while in the center of the room that doubled as dining and living room, trying to get a feel for the Stella he'd lost track of years before. What had happened to her since they'd last talked? Where had she gone? What had she done for four years? Who killed her? He thought maybe some of the answers had been in the room, but now might be with his boxes in Jerome Martin's office.

He learned quite a bit, though, in the next couple of hours, piling up papers and other things worth a closer look on the coffee table in front of the television, shoving aside an ashtray and an almost-empty glass of what looked like some kind of cola. Martin had left quite a bit, he thought, looking at the pile he ended up with.

He found two more address books, older ones, probably, than the one Martin had seized. Using the little portable scanner he'd purchased, he copied the pages from one of the books into the computer. He did the same with Stella's most recent telephone and cellular bills, taking a month of each. A wall calendar, prominently posted on a kitchen cabinet, had the previous Monday circled and a notation, "District Court."

He remembered that Stella had gotten into trouble again since he'd last seen her. Her checkbook showed payments made monthly to the Adult Probation Division for "restitution." A legal document from First Circuit Court warned her of a hearing date for motions on her Theft by Deception charge. It was dated 18 months earlier. A bill from her lawyer said she owed them $4,000.

Nothing jumped out at him, though. She'd lived simply, he thought. A few dishes in the cabinets, the refrigerator mostly empty. Even the bedroom closet was half empty, and so were the dresser drawers. He checked Martin's list again to see how much clothing he'd taken, counting only three items. Nothing in the apartment even hinted at a male presence.

When he'd scanned everything he thought he'd need, he went outside to see if anybody else had seen or heard anything of interest. He knocked on the doors of all of the fourth-floor apartments. People answered in two of them, including the one next door. No, they hadn't seen or heard anything last Sunday night. It had been very quiet. Yes, they'd told the same thing to the other detectives who asked. A Filipino woman two doors down said she saw Stella come home alone on Sunday afternoon. They were both parking their cars at the same time and rode up in the elevator together. This was, she thought, maybe five or 5:30. She didn't think Stella had gone back out again, because her car, a white Toyota, was still parked in the same place downstairs. She pointed it out to Rigg from the door.

Rigg went back to the apartment and dug through Stella's purse. Her driver's license still showed the old Kaneohe townhouse address, but the checks in the checkbook had Stella at the new place. The wallet held $35 and a pound of change. He found a big ring of keys, found a Toyota key, and rode the creaking elevator back down to the ground floor.

It didn't look like Martin had bothered to fingerprint the car. He went through the glove compartment, looked under the seats, and found nothing besides a form from Adult Probation for last week, Wednesday. She'd missed that appointment, too.

Back in the apartment, he packed up his things and looked around again. Martin's receipt fluttered in a little breeze on the table. A color photograph. He wondered where that had come from. He hadn't seen any pictures in the purse and went back into Stella's bedroom, finding an album of "Hawaiian Memories" on the dresser. The cover bore a picture of Diamond Head and a hula girl, and he started at the back with the most recent memories.

It was only half full, and most of the pictures in the album showed Stella and an older woman in various tourist attractions around Honolulu. They'd visited the Arizona Memorial, the Aloha Tower, Iolani Palace and a bunch of beaches. He thought Stella had some of the other woman's features, guessing maybe her mother had come out for a visit. All of the pictures had a date three years earlier printed in the lower right-hand corner. He flipped through the pages, coming to one holding only three photos. All were taken at the Kaneohe townhouse complex, which Rigg remembered clearly, and showed a group of men wearing blue jackets with yellow HPD markings, clustered around a white van in the parking lot. The view in the pictures was obviously that from the upstairs window of Stella's townhouse, the date stamp showing that they were taken on the day Rigg and the other task force officers seized Ray Streck's murder-mobile, as they called it. He recognized himself, standing with his back to the camera and pointing at something in the van. He wondered what the fourth picture had been of, and why Martin had taken that one and not any of the others. He suspected he might be featured in that one, too.

He leafed backward through the pages, stopping suddenly at one showing Stella and another, younger woman, part-Hawaiian, with brown hair and laughing brown eyes. This picture was different from all the others in the album. It was bigger, and overlapped two of the others, as though it had been stuffed down into the plastic protector sometime afterward. The color was slightly different, and Rigg thought it might have been taken by a different camera. It had no date stamp in the corner.

In the picture, two women were seated next to a man at a restaurant or a nightclub. All three were smiling at the camera, drinks on the table in front of them. Rigg slid the picture out of the plastic, carrying it over to the window to get a better look at it in the light. He turned it over, but there was no date on the back. He thought about scanning it, then put it in his pocket. He went more carefully through the album, finding no more pictures of the three, but stopping again on the page of three photos showing Streck's van, and took one of these, too.

He went back to the resident manager's apartment, finding the man watching a daytime soap and drinking a beer. The pressures of management didn't seem to be taking too great a toll. The manager heaved himself up off the couch at Rigg's knock and swayed over to the door, belching once. "Yeah?" he said.

"What kind of visitors did she have?" Rigg asked.

"You mean like men? Why, was she a hooker or something?" he leered. "She coulda been, I think. Kinda slutty, you ask me."

"No, I mean did anybody come over and visit with her, go to her place?"

"I don't know," he said. "Some local guy came by a few times. Big. Never stayed very long. That was a while back. Then some little dude with glasses, he came by once or twice in the last month or so. And there was another dude that came, mostly at night. She'd bring him in with her, they'd park and go up, and once I seen her taking him out again, pretty early in the morning. White guy, or mixed, kind of dark. Big. I figured maybe he was a relative or something, but now I think about it, maybe he was, like, a trick or something, 'cause he never stayed."

"What about Stella? Was she any trouble for you?"

"Nah. You practically never saw her. She came and went. Lots of nights, her space was the only one out there with no car in it. She probably had something going with somebody, sleeping over there. If she was tricking, she could've been sleeping anywhere."

That was about as helpful as the manager could be. He'd been watching a taped NFL game on Sunday night, and went to bed without seeing Stella or anybody else. Rigg asked what cars Stella's gentlemen callers drove.

"Hell, I don't know. We don't have no guest parking. They wanna visit, they park out on the street. I'll tow if I catch 'em in an assigned space."

Rigg asked if anybody in the building had been talking about what they'd seen or had told the police.

"Clarissa Kealoha. 3A. She works late someplace in Waikiki, was coming in that night, saw somebody. The other cops talked to her about it. She's been telling everybody. Can't shut her up." The manager waved off his thanks and headed back to the couch.

Rigg found Clarissa Kealoha, a waitress in one of the restaurants at the Hilton Hawaiian Village, getting dressed for her shift. Clarissa was happy to talk to more police officers about her big night. This was just about the most exciting thing that had ever happened to her and wasn't it a shame about Stella, who she'd never really met, but sounded like a really nice person, she said in a rush of words. When Rigg slowed her down, she said that she'd gotten home later than usual, almost 2:00 Monday morning, and saw the white van parked in a neighbor's stall.

"I don't think I was much help," she said. "I don't remember the license plate. They asked me if I saw any lettering or anything on the van, but I don't remember any."

"Did you see anybody in the van?"

"No. I told the other detective, there was nobody around. I remember thinking whoever it was, was gonna get towed, and they wouldn't be there to stop it."

"How about anywhere else? Did you see anybody else?"

"You mean, like strangers?"

"Yeah, or people that live here. That's pretty late. Was anybody still up and around?"

She thought about it. "There was a surfer. I remember thinking he was getting an early start."

"How did you know he was a surfer?"

"He had a surfboard in, like, one of those travel bags. Like you're gonna take your board to the mainland or Maui or someplace. One of those bags. I've got one like it, but I never go anywhere. He had the board in there. I told the detectives about him. He was coming into the building, and I remember thinking, 'oh, another surfer moved in.'"

"How big was this guy?"

"What are you, about 5'10"?"

"About that," Rigg said.

"This guy was bigger. I remember his head being closer to the top of the elevator."

"Could you identify him again if you saw him? Or if I showed you a picture?"

"I never really saw his face, mostly the side of him, but they came back and showed me some pictures already, on Thursday or Friday." She thought about it. "Friday. It was one of those things where they put in a whole bunch of pictures and you're supposed to pick out the one you saw. I didn't recognize anybody. I told them that."

Rigg thought that one over. If Martin was out showing witnesses photos, that meant he had a suspect already, though apparently not someone Clarissa Kealoha recognized.

He thanked her for her help and told her he might come back and bring more pictures for her to look at.

"I guess they use other policemen in those things, huh? Their pictures, I mean," she said.

"For the pictures in the photo spread? Sometimes. Mostly they're just other crooks who look something like the person we're investigating."

"You must look just like the guy, then," she said.

"I don't know, why?"

"Well, from what I remember, everybody looked kind of like you," and she picked up her car keys.

"Same height, same brown hair, same moustache. Yeah, and your picture was in there, too," she said. "I knew it as soon as I saw you."

Seventeen

Tuesday Afternoon

Rigg knew quite a bit more when he left than when he started, which is always a good thing in detective work. But when that happens, you usually come away with a lot more questions, and he had a few. These mostly centered on the picture now propped on his dashboard. Who took the picture? That was his first question. There were three people in it, but Rigg counted four drinks on the table. And if it was a man to make up two couples, who was he with, Stella or the other girl? He thought he knew the answer to that one, but it led to another, which was "what's he doing taking a picture of Stella Roddick and Ray Streck?" And finally, why were all of them sitting there with somebody who, if he was not mistaken, was the Double-crosser's very first victim?

Rigg remembered Carol Collins well, although they never met. When she was killed there hadn't even been a Double-crosser task force and Rigg was still assigned to Narco. HPD had treated Carol as a regular homicide, although she was a bad one, tortured, mutilated and stabbed to death. Not exactly the image the Hawaii Visitors Bureau wanted to project for the islands. The killer had dumped her nude body on the edge of Kaneohe Bay, about five miles from Streck's townhouse.

After a couple of days, Homicide didn't have any reasonable suspects, and the case went nowhere until a month later, when Amber Wheatley turned up dead on the other side of the island. The Chief called out the cavalry, unceremoniously yanking a dozen detectives out of other assignments, firing up the Double-crosser task force. One of the first things Rigg and the other detectives did then was to go over the complete case files for Carol Collins and Amber Wheatley, and he started with Carol. She'd been a lovely girl, a hapa haole, part-Hawaiian, part-Scottish, Norwegian and German. She had longish brown hair and expressive eyes that seemed to sparkle in the family photographs her aunt had shared. The pictures told of a girl who was happy in her life, maybe somebody trusting and loving and fun. The aunt who raised her after her mother died said Carol liked to surf and swim and she'd been looking for a clerical job when she went missing, needing something steady to support the baby born a year earlier.

Carol had a slightly darker side, though, a history of drug abuse, an abortion or maybe two, her aunt wasn't sure, and Narco said they had information she'd been dealing pot, ounces probably, and maybe a little crystal meth. Her aunt said she was in the process of breaking up with a guy she'd been seeing, whose name now escaped Rigg, but he was pretty sure it was on one of those disks in the Porsche's back seat. Whoever he was, the boyfriend had been the best lead, the Homicide detectives zooming in on him like heat-seeking missiles, but he had a very good alibi for the time of Carol's murder. He'd been locked up at the Halawa Medium Security Facility in Honolulu, awaiting bail on a robbery charge. After that, the investigation turned away and Carol Collins faded with it, swept away by the horror of seven more murders.

Well, she was back now, front and center. Rigg checked his watch. The sun was setting over Waikiki as he headed for Diamond Head. Time seemed to be flying by. He changed his mind and turned back toward Beretania Street and the police station. Things were getting complicated. His own police department was showing witnesses his picture at the victim's residence. And he'd gone to Stella Roddick's apartment with one murder to investigate and come away with two.

Eighteen

Tuesday evening

Rigg had the name now, Niko Blunt. He'd ducked into SUCS after the watch change, hitting his computer for every scrap of current information on Blunt, getting in and out without anybody seeing him. He assumed that they could track his computer searches through the mainframe, but hoped maybe they wouldn't pick up on his interest in Blunt right away.

He pulled the reports for Blunt's robbery conviction, writing down the names of some of the witnesses. Blunt got 10 years for that, with a four-year minimum term assigned by the Paroling Authority. Since Blunt had been incarcerated for those past four years, quite a few of the other records had dropped out of the system. He'd been the suspect in a domestic violence complaint made by Carol Collins, who had described herself as "girlfriend" in the report. It didn't look like this case had made it to trial, most likely because the Double-crosser butchered the complaining witness before she could testify.

Waikiki patrol had arrested Blunt for assault and ter-roristic threatening, the complainant saying Blunt had pushed him and "threatened to kick my ass and I believed him." A couple of DUI arrests and the contempt of court charges you get when you fail to answer a summons to appear in traffic court rounded out the rap sheet.

Rigg made up a list of all the addresses where Blunt had lived or worked, all the places he'd been arrested or come in contact with a police officer, intending to cross reference these with Stella and Streck. If he had time, he would also try to compare everything he had on Blunt with the eight Double-cross victims, especially the middle six, who were killed when Blunt's incarceration alibi didn't work.

When he was finished with Blunt, he plugged in the number from the Miscellaneous Crime Report Martin had taken from Stella's apartment. He wasn't particularly surprised to see that it related to her involvement in the Double-crosser case. Task force detectives had interviewed her several times, and he'd talked to her at least twice. In fact, according to the computer, the author of this particular report was none other than Ian Rigg. In the report, Rigg had documented his first face-to-face interview with Stella at the townhouse, getting her statement about the white van and her observations of Streck's comings and goings. He remembered giving her a copy of the statement a few days later when he'd gone back with the forms to apply for the Double-cross reward money. Martin had obviously found her possession of the report interesting enough to seize, but Rigg didn't see the connection to the murder. If Ed Chin was in the picture anywhere, and Rigg suspected he might be, he thought he'd probably find out the connection before too long.

Back at his house, with Kawika doing homework in his bedroom, he set up shop on the dining room table. He gulped down some extra-strength aspirins for the headache that wouldn't go away and began entering everything he'd found at Stella's and all of the Blunt information into his database. Then he did some basic searches to see if any connections jumped out at him, but nothing did.

He paid special attention to Blunt's alibi for the first and the last victims, trying once again but failing to shake the defense to those killings. For Carol Collins' murder, Blunt was locked up at the old Oahu Prison, which now held mostly people awaiting trial. Because it functioned as a jail, security at the facility was high, and Blunt hadn't made bail until a week after Collins was killed.

Once released, Blunt stayed out until a couple of weeks before Elaine Thomas turned up dead. At the time of her death, Blunt was doing his time in the Halawa Medium Security Facility, a large institution just west of Honolulu. In fact, the facility told the task force detectives that Blunt was still in the isolation wing that processed incoming inmates and assigned them to a facility when the murder took place. "He was in segregation," the corrections captain said. "For us, that's maximum security, and everybody goes there until we can figure out how dangerous he is, how he'll fit in, stuff like that." Not only did Blunt not leave the facility during the first month of his stay there, he received no visitors and had no access to the phone, "except to talk to his lawyer." Blunt could not have killed the prostitute Elaine Thomas, and Rigg didn't see how he could have killed his ex-girlfriend, Carol Collins, either. Did that rule him out for the other six? Rigg wore himself out thinking about this, constantly fiddling with the data he entered into the computer, trying new searches. Around 3:00 he decided he wasn't getting the answer this night and shut the computer down, calling it quits.

Emptying his pockets before bed, he pulled out a ring of unfamiliar keys. It took him a second to remember where he'd found them, finally picturing the purse in Stella's apartment. He'd been planning on taking them back upstairs after he talked to Clarissa Kealoha, but he must have been distracted. Her revelation that he was a key part of Jerome Martin's photo line-up would do it.

He threw the keys in a pile of the other evidence in the case, lying down on the couch and falling asleep almost immediately, even with the headache pain drumming in the background.

Nineteen

Wednesday morning

On Wednesday morning, Rigg dropped Kawika off at school, calling Sandy on the cell phone from the car to confirm that she'd be picking him up that afternoon and keeping him for the rest of the week. "Sorry," he told her. "But stuff's come up at work and I'll just be too busy," he said, hoping he still had police work to do next week.

He'd arranged to meet Silafau at Zippy's for breakfast, needing a favor and the chance to run some ideas past somebody who wouldn't report them back to Chin.

"So, you got some stuff out of the girl's place," Silafau said.

"Yeah, and I think I see how it went down. Stella gets home Sunday evening, she's in for the night. Her purse and keys and everything are still sitting there. Her car never moves. Sometime later, the killer comes up. Probably around midnight, maybe one or two. She lets him in, no problem, and before she knows it, it's over."

"She just let the guy in? No signs of forced entry?"

"Nothing. And no struggle in the apartment. Place looks fine. Maybe not real neat, but I think that was Stella's style. Kind of sloppy. And there wasn't that much stuff in the place, anyway. She was living cheap."

"But no struggle, it's got to be somebody she knows."

"At least somebody she trusts, to open the door up with no fuss at 1:00 in the morning. How many women living alone are gonna do that?"

"Is there a camera in the lobby? Do they have to buzz people up?"

"No. It's not that kind of place. They're lucky to have a freakin' elevator. You just go upstairs, knock on the door."

"Hey," Silafau said, looking like he'd just bitten into something sour. "You're not gonna want to hear this, but what if it was a cop? She'd open the door for a cop, wouldn't she?"

Sometime in the early hours of the morning, between typing on the laptop, popping more aspirin and brewing more coffee, the same thought had come to Ian Rigg. He rubbed tired eyes with both hands, thinking about the ramifications.

"Yeah, she would," he said finally. "Especially if it was a cop she knew already. Like me. I'll bet Martin and Chin already thought of that one, too. Martin's already been over there, showing my picture to the tenants. If any one of them said, 'Yeah, that looks like the guy,' that's gonna be it."

Silafau poured Rigg some coffee. "Well, we know it wasn't you, so who does that leave?"

"I don't know. She knew a couple other people on the task force. She probably talked to them more than me, but I think one's retired and I don't know where the other one's working now."

"You're gonna have to find out. Chin'll be narrowing it down, too. But what about other men who aren't cops? Can you figure out who else she might have known?"

"I think Martin got the most recent address book, but I got one that doesn't look too old. In fact, it might have been the one she was using back during the case. It's got my name and the task force number in it."

"Swell. And Martin passed it up?"

"If she's like me, she transferred the old numbers into the new book, so she might have put me in the latest version.

That would look even worse, since I haven't talked to her for four years."

"There must be other men in there."

"There are. I indexed 52. Some are only first names and phone numbers. Some have addresses and no numbers. I'm gonna have to do a background all of them."

"Fifty-two."

"Yeah, and there's no guarantee that our boy's in there."

Silafau chewed on his Portuguese sausage, finally putting aside the question of "who," moving on to "where." "What do you think, did he kill her there?"

"I don't know. Maybe. The neighbors said they didn't hear anything unusual, no banging around, no screaming. And Kamaka told me she died from one stab wound to the heart. The other stuff all happened post-mortem, so he could've killed her there and then done the cutting somewhere else."

"How did she get out of the apartment and over to your place?"

"She either walked, and nobody saw her, which is possible, but not likely, or the guy carried her out. I've got an idea about that, but I'm gonna talk to the ME, see if it holds water. Later today, I hope. If she went on her own steam, she was planning to come right back, because her house keys and her purse are both sitting on the kitchen counter. Either way, she didn't make a scene about it."

Silafau pondered that. "How do you think that picture fits in?"

Rigg pulled it out of his shirt pocket, dropping it on the table. "That's the weirdest thing. What's she doing in a picture with Streck and Carol Collins? I worked on that task force for a full year, and this picture is the only piece of evidence I've ever seen that shows any connection between Streck and one of his victims. That was the scariest thing about the Double-crosser. He was totally random. If you were the right type, he could pick you and rip you. There were no direct connections to him. Every single victim, we went over their lives with a microscope, looking for any possible link."

"That's hard to believe," Silafau said. "Knowing this place, where everybody's related to each other, everybody knows everybody else."

Rigg leaned over the table and closed his eyes, then opened them, focusing on the picture. "You remember that thing, Six Degrees of Separation? The theory that everybody in the whole world's connected to everybody else within six steps?"

"Yeah."

"Well, you're right. This is Honolulu. Everybody here's connected, and usually a lot closer than that. If they're not just flat-out related to you, it's stuff like where you take your car to be fixed, where you go to the doctor. Where you went to school, that's a big one. We had a big file on each victim, maybe a box of records for each one, and we're making connections, looking for something that puts them together or puts them together with somebody else. After we locked onto Streck, we went back and compared everything we dug up on him to the girls."

"And did you find any connections?"

Rigg laughed. "Hundreds. Thousands, maybe. Take the victims. One and six went to the same school. Three and five went to the same hairdresser. Two and four both used to work at the same place. Three, five and seven all drove Hondas. Stuff like that. Is that important, or is it nothing? It drove us nuts. And the same thing for Streck. We found possible ties, but nothing that stood right up and shouted at you." He held up the picture, pointing to Carol Collins and Ray Streck. "And right there, that's the closest we can put a victim and the killer together."

"Jeez. How come Martin never took the picture when he was doing his search?"

"He only came to Homicide a year or two ago. He didn't know Streck, although he might have seen a picture, but he definitely didn't know Collins, not like we all did. There were a lot of pictures of Stella in there, and other women. I went back through and looked after I found this, but this was the only victim. I think he just missed it."

"You found a connection; what are you going to do?"

"Whoever took this picture is the key now." Rigg tapped the empty place at the table and the drink in front of it. "Streck's dead, Collins is dead, Stella's dead. Whoever took the picture, if they're still alive, is the only one left. Whoever it is knew all three people, he's got to have some of the answers."

"You think it's a he?"

"Yeah, I do. There's two drinks, look like margaritas on the table, a beer and what might be a rum and coke or something like it. I think it's a man's drink, and he'd fill out two couples."

Silafau peered at the picture. "You can't even tell where it was taken."

"Or when. Like how long before Carol Collins got ripped was she sitting there with Streck? Could've been that night. That's a good question. What did she have in her stomach when they found her? I wonder if I can get the autopsy report."

"Shoot, man. You keep coming up with more questions, you're gonna be at this thing a long damn time."

"I know it," Rigg said. "Only I don't think I've got that much time left. And I need to ask for a favor."

Silafau was happy to help out. "Anything to move this thing along," he said.

"Thanks, man," Rigg said. "What I need is some information from inside the joint at Halawa. That's where this guy,

Blunt, was locked up. I need to know about him and if I ask them directly, I'm gonna get that 'there's nothing to see here, folks' bullshit you get from the Corrections people. If they think something's gonna come back on them, they'll cover their own asses. I don't have enough time to deal with that crap right now. I don't care if it's a corrections officer or an inmate, as long as they're not hiding anything."

"I can probably find somebody," Silafau said. "A lot of the A.C.O.s are Samoan, and there's plenty of Samoan inmates, unfortunately."

"Okay. I'll meet them anywhere within reason. And tell 'em, it's strictly off the record."

"I'll get something by this afternoon."

"Thanks," Rigg said. "Call me on my cell phone. I've got to go to Kailua to talk to somebody."

Twenty

Wednesday morning

Moaniala Collins still lived in the same little Kailua cottage where she had raised her sister's child so many years before. Rigg walked through the neat yard and up two steps to the front lanai, taking in the usual collection of rubber slippers lined up next to the door. Judging from the sizes, there were still some small feet in the Collins house.

"Yes," she said, welcoming him into the house. "This is where Carol grew up. I'm surprised anyone still remembers, she's been away so long. You call me Auntie Moani, like she did."

"I'm just following up on some old cases, and her name came up," Rigg said, taking the offered seat.

"They told me they caught that man, the one who took her away."

"Well, we didn't exactly catch him. He died first, but we're sure he took Carol. I wanted to show you a picture. Carol's in it. Is that going to upset you too much?"

"No, of course not," she said, smiling. "She's alive in your picture?"

"Yes, ma'am."

"And she's still alive, here," she said, holding one hand over her heart. "I see a picture of Carol, I remember her the old way. I feel her here."

"Okay," Rigg handed her the photograph, watching her cradle it, seeing her smile again.

"Oh, yes. Doesn't she look happy? It's good to see her that way."

"Yes, ma'am. I think she was happy there. But can you tell me who these people are? The other two."

Auntie Moani examined the images of Streck and Roddick. "The man, I never saw him, I don't think. The woman, did she drive a, what do you call them? Like a Jeep thing."

"An SUV? I don't know."

"I think I saw her one time. She had a blue Jeep thing, it didn't have a top, just metal around it like a blue cage. And she was driving right down the street here, with Carol. Going that way," she pointed up toward the Koolau mountain range. "Mauka. There were some friends, I don't know if I would call them that, of Carol's who lived back there, toward the end of the street. Trouble. I don't like seeing her spending time with them, but she's a big girl, now." She put the picture down on the table, looking up toward the mountains, quiet for a moment, sighing, then picking it back up.

"And I waved at Carol, but she didn't see me. They were up there a little while and then they came back. I waved again, and Carol told this girl," she tapped Roddick's image, "told her to stop, and she got out and gave me a big hug, and said this was her friend, and they were going into town."

"How long was this before … before Carol went away?"

Carol's auntie handed the picture back. "Not long. In fact, I think that might have been the very last time I've seen her. Is that useful to you?"

"It's very helpful. You have a good memory. I don't think I could remember something like that, four years ago."

"If it really was the last time, then I'm sure it would stay with me," Auntie Moani smiled. "Do you have any more pictures?"

"Yes, actually, I have one. Not of Carol, though." He got out Blunt's mug photo, handing it to her. "Do you remember him?"

Moaniala Collins made a face. "Aiee. Such trouble, this one. So bad for Carol, but she doesn't listen. She loves him, she says."

"You know him."

"Niko. I told the detectives before, back when Carol went away. I said, 'Look at this man, he could have hurt her,' but they told me he was in prison already. I said, 'Good for him, I hope he stays there.' Is he still in prison?"

"Yes. He's been there more than four years. How was he bad to Carol?"

"Oh, she came over here, saying he was going to leave her. There was another girl. I told her, 'Good thing he's leaving. Let the other girl have him. Too bad he took so long.' She told me she loves him and he's the baby's father, and she was going to try to get some money from him for the baby. Child support. But he wasn't paying and she asked me if I could give her some money. I asked her, how come if this person loves you, he won't take care of you and the baby? She told me I'm old and I don't understand." She put Blunt's picture down and picked up the other one. "She was right about that. I didn't understand, and I don't."

"Did she go to the State to get any child support money from him?" Rigg said.

She shook her head. "No. I don't think she would have pressed him. I think she was telling him, 'Okay, you want to leave? Fine, it's going to cost you. Better you stay.' I think she thought that would keep him. Maybe he killed her because of it."

Rigg saw the tears starting, heard the pain in her voice, felt a little of the doubt that had wracked her for four years. "I don't think it mattered," he said. "If he was in prison, she was safe from him. This other girl, could she have been the one in the picture? The one with the blue Jeep?" he said, not changing the subject, exactly, but moving away from the heart of it.

"I don't know. I think Carol left maybe a week after that. Maybe only a few days. I never found out any more."

He looked around the house, thinking of the little boy whose mother had been taken away, remembering the little slippers at the front door. "What happened to her son?" he asked.

Auntie Moani smiled through the tears. "Oh, he'll be home from kindergarten soon. Carol was my hanai daughter," she said, using the Hawaiian word for an adoption, usually one within a family. "And I took in little Zachary, too, after. We're all ohana, and we have to look after each other."

Rigg asked a couple more questions, gave her an old card with his new numbers written in, then walked to his car. In the front seat, he took out the second picture he'd found in Stella's apartment, looking at himself in the parking lot with the white van. Parked in a stall at the bottom of the picture closest to Stella's townhouse was a blue Jeep Wrangler, with no roof and a roll bar that looked like a blue cage.

Wednesday afternoon

"Medical Examiner's office, Kawamoto."

"Danny? This is Kimo Rigg. How are you doing?"

"Kimo, nice to hear from you."

"Yeah. You probably heard I'm back at the PD, working out of the Unsolved Crimes Section."

"Yes, we heard. Congratulations."

"Thanks. Hey, I've got a question on a homicide last week. Can you check a detail for me?"

"Probably. Let's see if it's in the computer. Who's the victim?"

"Stella Roddick. White female. She was 34."

"I remember. She looked a lot like your old case, didn't she? We were talking about that down here."

"Yeah. I was kind of spooked when I heard." Rigg said.

"What did you want to know?"

"She was nude when we found her, but did she have anything on her body or in her hair? Residue or fibers?"

The line hummed quietly for a few seconds while the doctor read the report. "Kimo?" he said. "No fibers visible, but they'd vacuum for that and check later. It doesn't say here."

"How about wax, maybe some sand? Anything like that?"

There was a pause, the doctor asking him, "Were you there at the scene?"

"I saw her there but I stayed outside the tape."

"I don't know how you'd know that, then," Kawamoto said. "The report does say there was a waxy substance and sand. Posterior only. On the back of her arms and legs and in her hair. Also marks consistent with restraint with some kind of wide tape. They took swabs and the crime lab's testing for the type of tape. How did you know?

"You know me; I was always a lucky guesser. Were there any other signs of force or injuries? I know about the cuts. Besides those."

"There don't appear to be any."

"What about drugs in the system?"

"They did the routine toxicology screen, but I don't see the results here, yet," Kawamoto said. "I can call you when we get them."

"How about cause? Kamaka told me she got one stab wound to the heart."

"No, that was post mortem, same as the other injuries. She went by MAMI." Kawamoto said.

"Mammy? What the hell is that?"

"Massive Acute Myocardial Infarction. She had a heart attack. Sudden and fatal."

Rigg actually held the cell phone away from his ear and looked at it in surprise, the words were so unexpected. "Heart attack," he said, putting it back to his ear. "But you are still calling this a homicide …"

"Oh, yes. Death at the hands of another. And the stab wound would have done it if the heart attack didn't. I'll tell you, we don't see this very often, but it looks like whoever had the knife basically frightened her to death."

"You're kidding."

"No. And I don't know who you're looking at for this, but I'd be careful. This is one very scary character."

Rigg gave his work and cell phone numbers, thanked him and hung up, the picture a bit clearer, but puzzling over the cause of death. Stella was only 30 and not in any of the obvious risk categories for a heart attack. He had to agree with Kawamoto. Whoever had killed Stella must be one very scary character.

TWENTY-ONE

WEDNESDAY AFTERNOON

Bear Akana answered the phone at Adult Probation and sounded happy to hear from his teammate. "Sure, I'll find out for you," he said, when Rigg asked him for information about Stella and Blunt. "Let me get the spellings. Do you want to talk to their P.O. if they're on probation now?"

"Probably," Rigg said.

"Stella's dead, which I guess you probably knew already," Bear said when he called back. "I'll give you the number of her P.O. Blunt's technically still locked up on the old robbery charges, but he's at Kalihi now, the work release center. He gets out during the days for work and has to be back by seven every night. What else do you need to know?"

Rigg thought about it. "Can you get his employer's name for me? And when he gets out of work release, is he going to be on parole, or what?"

"He's working for ZNT Construction; they're masonry contractors. And when he gets out, he'll actually be on parole, which is handled by another office. Stella was on five years' probation for theft. She had four to go. Her file's with us. She used a forged credit card to buy a bunch of stuff at stores down in Waikiki. Had to pay restitution and a $1,000 fine, too."

"Thanks, man. That's really helpful. Is there anything in her file that shows a connection to Blunt, or would her P.O. know that?"

"There's nothing on the computer, but I don't have her file. You should ask Ferreira, he had her case. I'll transfer you over. See you at practice."

Rigg got a little more from Joe Ferreira, who had found out his client was dead when Martin called last Monday afternoon. According to Ferreira, Stella had been a model probationer, no trouble, always passed the drug screens, even the surprise ones.

"I did a couple of spot checks on her at her apartment in the last couple of months since I inherited her case," he said. "That was about six months ago. Never found anything to revoke her on, or even have a hearing."

"What about this guy, Blunt?" Rigg asked. "Is there anything in the file about him?"

"I don't see anything. Is he a felon?"

"Yeah. He's in work release now, according to Bear. Robbery case."

"Well, she shouldn't be associating with him. That would be a violation. Same thing would go for him, so if they were seeing each other, I'd be the last person she'd tell."

"Not allowed any contact at all?"

"No association with other felons. It's one of the conditions the court sets. She had to agree to it if she wanted to stay out of prison. The only exception is if they're married or related."

"Would she get revoked for that?"

"Probably not for a first offense. We'd warn her and monitor."

"One other thing, do you have any other addresses where she might have been staying?"

Rigg could hear Ferreira flipping through the papers. "No," he said. "That apartment was it, why?"

"Because I was in the place, and I don't know, but to me, it didn't look lived in. Not much food, only a couple of dishes. And do you know any women with one closet and it's half empty? 'Cause I don't."

"You think she had another place?"

Rigg remembered the key ring he'd accidentally taken from the apartment. There did seem to be a lot more keys than you'd need for that place and a 10-year-old Toyota. "I'll let you know if I find it," he said.

He got Ferreira's direct line and said he'd call back if he got anything else new on Stella. "Don't bother," Ferreira told him. Stella Roddick no longer owed anything to the Adult Probation Division of the State of Hawaii, but if he had any more questions, he should feel free to call. "Bear gave me two more case files this morning. I don't need to waste any more time on the dead ones," he said.

"Okay. Can you give me back to Bear?"

A minute later, Akana was back on the line. "Yeah, Kimo?"

"One more question. What does your man Ferreira look like?"

"Short little local guy, with glasses. Why?"

"The manager at Stella's apartment described somebody like that, and Ferreira said he met her at her place a couple of times."

"That's his job. She must've been clean, 'cause he never filed any violation reports that I saw."

"Okay, well, I'll see you at practice. And thanks," Rigg said.

"Shoot. And you get to the bottom of this thing. I'm glad they gave you something important to do after all."

Wednesday afternoon

The call from Amy Fraga at CID sent Rigg back down to the station. Major Hata wanted to get a progress report on the tagging case. Rigg thought maybe he owed the major an apology over the Double-crosser file and started off saying he was sorry for the trouble, but Hata had a different take on it.

"Shut the door, will you?" he said. "Don't worry about it, I took care of it."

"What do you mean? I figured Chin would get all wild about me asking for it."

"Nah, I told him it was my idea. I said I'd been looking for a place for the files for a while, which was true, and I wanted somebody from the old task force to go through it and see if we should keep it around or permanently archive it. There's only about three people from the task force still in the department and you and Kamaka are the only ones working for me. Kamaka's busy and you're not, so …"

Rigg sat back, surprised. "Gee, thanks. I thought you were gonna get in all kinds of trouble over me. I've been thinking about how I was going to explain it."

"No need worry. Now, before I ask you about the other thing, how's OZ MAN 1 going? Chin does want to know about that." Hata pulled out a pen and a notepad.

Rigg described his investigation so far, covering the interviews and the fruitless surveillances, concluding that it was probably going to take a few more sleepless nights before he could catch the elusive tagger. "And even when I get him, the prosecutor isn't going to charge him with much. It feels like a waste of time."

"It is, but are you going to get him?" Hata said.

"Yeah. I think so," Rigg said. "Now that somebody's on his ass full-time, it comes down to the old cops and robbers game. He's got to be lucky every night. I've only got to get lucky once. Sooner or later my number's coming up."

Hata looked up from his notes. "Chin's asking me for daily progress reports. I don't care what you give me, but write something up that describes your leads, interviews, whatever.

I'll just forward it to him. Just email it to me every day, that should do it."

"Okay."

"Now, tell me where you are on the other thing."

"What other thing?"

"The Roddick murder. What else?" Hata put his pen away and shoved the notes to one side of the desk. They were off the record. "Don't look so shocked. I'm not stupid. You wanted the files for a reason."

The two of them stared at each other for a minute, Rigg finally deciding to feel the thing out. "I don't know. I've been thinking for a few days maybe I was the suspect in this deal, that you were looking at me."

"I'm not, but they are." He jerked his thumb at the ceiling. "It's being run out of Chin's office. He's got people from CIU and Internal Affairs working on it, and he's got Martin reporting directly to them. I'm officially out of the loop. Let's see how they put it." He pulled a piece of HPD stationery out of a pile on the desk and scanned it. "Right, 'due to the sensitive and confidential nature of the investigation,' which pisses me off royally. I know what's going to happen, they go off chasing the wild goose, sure as hell it's going to be an unsolved homicide on my stat sheet this year." Hata tossed the paper back onto the pile.

"Yeah, well, to be honest with you, your stat sheet isn't my biggest problem right now," Rigg said. "I'm more worried they're gonna decide to show it as Cleared By Arrest, and the arrest they make'll be me, even if they can't prove it."

"It could happen," Hata said. "Which pisses me off even more, because you work for me, and how is that going to look? So, what do you know?"

"I'm not very far along. I've got how and when, and probably where, but I'm a long way from who and why."

"What's how and when?"

"How's pretty strange. I guess you heard the cause of death is a heart attack, huh?"

"Yeah. Scared her to death, then stabbed and cut her. Martin told me that much, before he got detoured."

"Right, well, I think that all happened in the van, after 2:00 on Monday morning. I think the killer goes up to her place sometime after midnight. She lets him in, no fuss, no muss. She either knows him or trusts him enough to open the door. He's a big guy, he overpowers her."

"No signs of force used on her."

"No. So how did he get her to submit? Don't know. Have to make that a question. Anyway, he's got her, unconscious, I think, and he tapes her up to a surfboard." Rigg said.

"A surfboard? How do you know that?"

"Because, she's got wax and sand on the backs of her arms and legs, and in her hair. It's not on the front of her, like it would be if she got it surfing and she was laying face down on the board. And there's none on her back or her butt, so she was probably still dressed."

Hata nodded, visualizing it.

"She's got tape marks on her, so he tapes her to the board. Now, does he kill her there, or somewhere else? She could've had the heart attack there in the apartment. Martin didn't find anything there, at least not that he put on his receipt. No visible bloodstains on the furniture or the clothes, but if she really had a heart attack and all the knife work was after she was dead, there wouldn't be much bleeding. But I think the cutting probably didn't happen there at her place. He took her away from the scene, stripped her down somewhere else, or just did her in the van."

"How did he get her away from the apartment?"

"In one of those travel bags you put your board in when

you go through the airport. He's got her all quiet or dead, waits till nobody's around, then slings her over his shoulder and walks her down to the van. One of the residents saw somebody she didn't know taking a bag like that into the building about 2:00 when she got off work."

"Does that fit with the time of death?"

"Yeah, the time of death is supposed to be around 3:00 a.m., that's what Kamaka said, and I didn't see her getting dumped until 4:30. They leave the building at 2:30, she expires at 3:00, give or take half an hour or so. That's still a long time to be driving around town with a dead body in your car, though."

"You'd have to be pretty strong to pull that off, too."

"Yeah, Stella goes 130 or 135, plus the surfboard and the bag. The guy's got a 150 pounds over his shoulder. He can push some weight. He's big and he's somebody Stella knows or trusts. He's got a white van, a surfboard and a travel bag. He knows the Double-crosser's M.O., or at least some of it, and he's a strong son of a bitch."

Hata made a few more notes. "You don't fit any of those except the M.O. part. No offense, but I don't think you could do that thing with the surfboard."

"No, I know the Double-crosser M.O., but the rest of it doesn't work."

"So, you're off the hook. You got anybody who fits?"

"Niko Blunt. He's good for everything except for the Double-crosser's M.O. How would he know that? I don't know. But he works for a contractor, so he might have access to a van, he's big, 6'3", weighs 220, and he's been locked up for the last four years. I'm gonna be talking to the prison people, see if they remember him, but I bet they're gonna say he spent his exercise time pumping iron in the yard. He sounds like the type."

"What have you got putting Blunt with Roddick?"

"I'm working on it. I'm down to one step away, but I'm not there yet. I'll tell you what I can do, though. I can put Roddick together with Carol Collins, one of the Double-cross victims, and with Ray Streck. And I can put Collins with Niko Blunt. That's a pretty tall coincidence."

"Collins was which victim?"

"Number one. But Niko got popped for a robbery he did in Kailua, and when Carol was killed, he was locked up at Halawa. He made bail eventually, but he pled out and got sentenced before the last of the killings. He's finishing up his five-year minimum, now."

"What was his connection to Collins?"

"Boyfriend-girlfriend, it sounds like. They had a kid together. But they might have had some other stuff going on. He might've been supplying her with ice. From what I can tell, they were both dealing at the time. And Collins' aunt says some other girl was trying to get Carol's boyfriend while Collins was pushing Blunt for child support. One big, happy family."

"Hmmm," Hata gazed up at the ceiling. "And you've got Streck and Collins together with Roddick?"

Rigg pulled out the picture, putting it on Hata's desk. "There they are. The picture shows for sure that Stella didn't tell us everything. She knew Streck better than she said. And it shows that Carol wasn't just a random victim. Streck knew her. Well enough to be out painting the town with her."

"I'm not going to ask where you got the picture. Is it going to hold up in court?"

Rigg shook his head. "Maybe, but who are we gonna prosecute? Everybody in the picture's dead. No way to show Blunt took it, or anybody else, for that matter."

"But if Blunt and Streck knew each other, that might explain how Blunt knew the Double-crosser's M.O."

"We're getting close. You could say the exact same thing for Stella."

"Yeah, what about Stella? Did she ever talk about Streck with you?"

"No, damn it," Rigg said. "That's been bugging me, too. Why in the hell did she lie? Her statement was that she knew this guy from the complex and talked to him a couple of times in the parking lot, but that was it. She never said anything about partying with him, and she definitely never said she knew Carol Collins. That'd be awful hard to forget, since Carol's name and picture were in the paper with the other girl's practically every day."

"Yeah, that's kind of suspicious, right there." Hata said.

"You bet it is. In fact, I'd rate that an out-and-out lie, because I know I asked her at some point if she'd had any other contact with Ray."

Rigg looked at the picture again. "Blunt. I've got to talk to him, but I'll tell you one thing, if I find out he was out of his bed at the work release program on Monday morning, he's gonna look awful good for this thing."

Hata smiled. "I'm glad somebody looks good for it besides you. But I can't stop them coming after you, you know. I probably won't even know beforehand if they decide to go for a warrant."

"I know it," Rigg said. "I think I've got about another day and a half."

"You'd better get busy, then," Hata said. "Because if they do come after you, you're gonna be on your own."

Wednesday evening

He didn't want to be on his own, the familiar feeling of isolation making his new house a prison. But when Iwa called, wanting to know if she could come over with dinner that night, he told her no. "IA will be at the bottom of the driveway. I'm not dragging you into this deal." She said she didn't care, but he told her maybe he could see her Saturday, hoping she wouldn't be looking at him through a set of steel bars.

The call from Silafau came in at six, Rigg's cell phone going off just as he was helping pull the canoe up onto the launching ramp.

"Can you get over to Zippy's in Kahala, the big one? The guy from the prison's gonna be there at 6:30," Nate said.

"I'll be there. How am I going to know him?"

"He'll be the biggest Samoan in the place."

And Sergeant F. Tuisuga was, indeed, one of the largest Samoans Rigg had ever seen. "Falefasa Tuisuga," the man said, holding out a surprisingly gentle hand. "Call me 'Fasa.' I hear you want to know about Niko Blunt."

"Yeah. Did Nate tell you why?"

"Oh, he said the boy was in trouble. I told him, he's an inmate, what else is new?"

Tuisuga worked at the Halawa Medium Security Facility. "Blunt was in my module for three years. I saw him every day," he said.

"First off, tell me he was a weightlifter …"

"Yeah, he worked out. He did the weights, resistance training, the whole bit."

"Was he in trouble a lot?"

"He spent some time in the SHU—Special Holding Unit. Talking back to the officers and stuff. Nothing real serious."

"What about visitors? Did he get any?"

"Hmmm. Some girl came by on weekends. Haole girl. That all stopped a year or so ago. I didn't see her after that, and then he went to work release. That was the last I saw him, too."

Rigg got out the picture, handing it to Tuisuga. The snapshot disappeared into his huge hands. "You see her there?"

"That's her." He touched Stella's face. "She came pretty regular. I took him down to visiting, she'd be there."

"Did he talk about why she stopped coming? Were they having problems?"

Tuisuga thought about it, looking at the picture. "I don't think so," he said, finally. "He was behaving himself, being pretty good, getting ready for work release, staying out of trouble. She might've had some trouble, though. We get that. Inmate's wife or girlfriend gets busted for something, she can't pass the security screen anymore. No more visits. That could've happened with her."

"Yeah, she got convicted on a theft charge about a year or a year and a half ago, got put on probation."

"That'd do it. They do a rap check on the visitors. If she's on probation, she can't come in. He might've still been talking to her on the phone, though."

Rigg got the picture back. "He had access to a phone?"

"Sure. Payphone on the tier. They make collect calls to the outside. As long as she's got a phone, and she'll take his calls, he can get her when it's his phone time."

Tuisuga said there would be records of every visit Stella made to the facility, and something in Blunt's file listing all the visitors he was authorized to receive. "He's got an approved visitors list. I'll check tomorrow and see if her name's on it."

"Stella Roddick," Rigg told him. "But if you can get me all the names on the list, that'd be even better." He gave Tuisuga his cell phone number and said he'd wait for the call.

"Sure. But let me tell you. You're going after this man? Watch yourself."

"Why is that?"

Tuisuga tapped his spoon against the table, thinking for a minute. "Some men, in prison, they just want to be left alone, do their time, get out, maybe they come back, maybe not. They're the sheep. Others, like Blunt, they're the wolves. He's big, he's in shape and he's got the attitude, up here." He tapped the spoon against the side of his head. "He sees people as something to hunt, and he's gonna find a way to get what they've got. Doesn't matter if it's a cigarette or a girl, he's hunting. Even the A.C.O.s, I see him watching us, thinking, 'Can I take him?' Watch yourself."

"Okay, I will."

Tuisuga stood, towering over the table. "He told me one time, 'I love it in here.' Man like that, he's not like you or me."

Rigg headed off for his OZ MAN 1 stakeout in a positive mood. Somebody had finally put Niko Blunt and Stella Roddick together, face to face.

Wednesday evening/Thursday morning

OZ MAN 1 had not returned to the scene of his crime on Tuesday night or early Wednesday morning. With over 300 different locations in play, Rigg figured the odds of catching this person by stake-out were pretty poor. And OZ MAN 1 could always go someplace new, making the odds even longer. Rigg spent the evening at the fire station again, mulling over the tagger's M.O. and looking for an opening that would give him a little edge. Around midnight, he thought he had found it.

Looking again at the photographs of OZ MAN 1's work, something new jumped out at him and he shuffled them into three piles, one for each of the tagger's primary styles. OZ MAN 1 had three distinct "tags." The first was the looping O Z scrawl he used on small signs, fire hydrants, a door, or a bus stop bench. Made with either a wide-tip marker pen or a can of spray paint, he could probably lay down this tag in two or three seconds. Rigg thought OZ MAN 1 probably dropped these tags on his way to or from his more elaborate creations, or just when he felt the urge.

The second type of tag also featured the O Z signature, but was more intricate and creative. Rigg found these on public and private property, including the wall of the very fire station he was staking out. These paintings covered more area, had more than one color, and took some time to do right, though probably not more than a few minutes. This pile of pictures was considerably smaller than the first, though still substantial.

The last pile, though, had only 15 photographs, each of these of the large wall murals that were obviously OZ MAN 1's pride and joy. With several colors and loads of imagination, Rigg thought, these must take hours to create, and some would take all night. A couple occupied space on walls 40 feet long and eight feet high, an almost 400-square-foot advertisement for idle hands and misdirected youth. OZ MAN 1 spent some money on these projects, too, laying on the spray paint in vivid displays of line and color. One or two had the O Z label incorporated into the painting, but most held some other message and were almost lovingly signed "OZ MAN 1" down in the corner, as an artist would do.

He looked up at the fire station wall, still empty of fresh graffiti in the moonlight. It was a nice wall, facing a large intersection and a church parking lot. Your message would certainly be visible on that wall, but no one could possibly finish one of OZ MAN 1's masterpieces in such exposed conditions in one night. The specials, as Rigg decided to call them, were all placed in slightly out-of-the-way locations, usually above the normal line of sight. In the daytime, your eyes would be drawn up to OZ MAN 1's splash of fresh color on a building or sign, but at night, following the beams of your headlights in the darkness, you wouldn't see the creation taking shape just out of view.

If you want to hurt OZ MAN 1, Rigg thought, you go after one of these icons. He started his car and drove to a nearby service station, parking under the light and examining the police reports connected to the masterpiece locations. Some of the specials had been painted over as many as three times, but OZ MAN 1 always returned within a few days to imprint his new artistic vision on the space. He always came back. This, Rigg thought, had possibilities. He put the reports and the pictures in one pile and headed for Diamond Head. Behind him, two pairs of headlights snapped on, cars easing onto the empty street behind Rigg.

Maybe somebody should have stayed at the fire station, because sometime between four and five on Thursday morning, OZ MAN 1 tagged the wall again.

Twenty-Two

Thursday morning

The Kalihi Work Release Center is across the street and around a corner from Honolulu's oldest prison. When you're almost ready to get out of the one place, they put you in the other one. "It's called transitioning into the community," the facility administrator told Rigg on Thursday morning. "The residents have to be working, and they have other rules to follow, but it's all designed to get them back into society, one step at a time."

There's a fence around the Kalihi WRC, but it's not one of those serious ones that really aspire to keep people in or out. "It's more of a symbolic thing," the administrator said. "But if they cross it when they're not supposed to, they're considered escapees," just like if they climbed over those serious and non-symbolic razor wire models across the street.

As of Wednesday morning, Niko Blunt was listed as one of those escapees. "He didn't return from his work by seven on Tuesday. We're flexible up to a point," the administrator said. "People miss buses or can't get parking, but they're supposed to call, and he didn't. It usually takes a day or two, but there'll be a warrant for escape issued by tomorrow morning."

"It's too bad, too," said Blunt's case manager. "He was doing okay. Up for parole in three more months. Now he's got to go back across the street when they catch him."

"For how long?" Rigg asked.

"Oh, he'll have to finish out his original sentence, which was 10 years, and they may add on three more for escape."

"Whoa," Rigg said. "He must've had some really urgent business somewhere else."

The administrator and the case manager nodded, both giving him their grave and concerned faces. "And if we can ask, or if you can tell us," the administrator said. "Why are you asking about Blunt?"

Rigg wondered what their reaction would be if he told them he thought Blunt had murdered somebody while he was supposed to be locked safely away behind the symbolic fence. He didn't think they were going to be too happy. "Let me ask you first, was he here on Sunday night? Or early Monday morning. Before five a.m."

Now they stopped looking concerned, trading one of those shifty glances you usually get when some civil service employee you're confronting is going into his C.Y.A. mode.

"Of course he should have been here," the case manager said. "He's supposed to be here between seven and seven. Everybody with a job checks out at seven in the morning."

Rigg noted that this explanation did not answer his question, and pointed this out.

"Well, our, uh, monitoring during the evening hours is, uh. Not completely adequate, should we say?" the administrator said. "There's only one person on duty at night, and he's at the front desk in the lobby."

"It sounds a little like a hotel," Rigg said. "Where the guests check in and check out and come and go as they please."

"We rely on trust. The honor system, in a way," the administrator said, looking at the case manager, who backed him up with vigorous nodding, reminding Rigg of one of those dashboard hula dolls on a bumpy road. "These are residents who are already classified as return-ready," the case manager said. "They're getting out soon; they don't have any reason to break the rules."

"But they do break the rules," Rigg said. "This guy did when he didn't come back the night before last. What I want to know is, was he out some other time when he wasn't supposed to be? You tell me you're dead certain he was here between midnight and 4:30 a.m. on Monday, and I'm out of your hair."

"He could have been out," the case manager sighed. "We do a bed check at 10 and then the night man is supposed to spot check during the night …" He looked away. "He's supposed to stay awake, but …"

"I got it," Rigg said. "If I ask him, he'll swear on his mother's grave that everybody was here, sleeping like little babies. But what you're telling me is, as long as Blunt got back in time to check out for work on Monday morning, he could've been anywhere after 10."

The administrator and the case manager looked at each other, then back at Rigg. They didn't say anything, not denying it.

"Okay. I'm gonna have to talk to the night man anyway."

"But why would Blunt take such a big risk when he's going to be released in just a couple of months?" the case manager said.

"I'm not sure," Rigg said. "But he might have had somebody he wanted to kill. And you folks make an awfully good alibi."

Thursday morning

They called the night man at home, and just as Rigg suspected, he vouched for every one of his charges, denying that he'd taken even a short nap during the after-midnight hours. Convinced the man was lying but with no easy way to prove it, Rigg put the work release center on the back burner.

And ZNT Construction went to the front. Their offices

were also in Kalihi, in an industrial area not far from the prison. The foreman didn't seem surprised to see Rigg.

"I been expecting you guys. I hope you're gonna tell me you found my truck," he said, when Rigg showed him the gold detective badge.

"What truck?" Rigg said.

"A white 1995 Ford Econoline van with 180,000 miles on it. Looks just like that one, right there." He pointed to another van with the ZNT logo on the door. The van had rectangular taillights and a license plate offset to the right. "I told you guys on the phone yesterday morning it was stolen. One of your uniform people came by and took a report," the manager said.

"Oh, really? A white van? You got any ideas about who took it?"

"Hell, yes. Niko Blunt. Employee. Ex-employee, now. He drove it regular, had the keys. Took it out Tuesday to work, never brought it back. Son of a bitch was 10 years old, but it still did the job. The van, not Blunt, he's more like 34."

According to the foreman, Blunt walked over every morning from the work release center, got his assignment and took the van to the worksite, returning it every night in time to walk back. "They're only a couple of blocks from here," the foreman said. "He'd always show up right before seven, jog back over to the facility. Cutting it close."

"But he kept the keys?"

"Yeah. It speeds things up in the morning. Our office people aren't always here by seven, so if he knows where he's working that day, he can just pick up the van and take it out. There's a lock on the gate there, but he's got a key on the ring for that, too."

"So, what you're telling me is, if he wanted to use the van during the night, he could come over here and get it," Rigg said.

The foreman nodded. "Sure. As long as it was back in the morning, we wouldn't know it was gone. But he's locked up over there at the work release place. He's not supposed to be out at night."

"I know," Rigg said. "That's what everybody keeps telling me. Let me get the info on your van."

The foreman gave him the license number and the description, then asked, "Hey, if you didn't come over about my van, why are you here?"

"You guys are masonry contractors, right? You do walls?"

"All kinds of walls," the foreman said. "Rock, brick, hollow tile, you name it, we'll put it up. You need a wall built?"

"No, actually, I wanted to ask about this guy." Rigg pulled out a packet of pictures of OZ MAN 1's special creations. "I'm working on a tagging deal. We've gotten a ton of complaints about him."

The foreman riffled through the pictures. "Yeah, I think I've seen his stuff. He's all over the place. We've been hit at a bunch of our jobs. The little bastards do like walls. I don't know if it was this guy, but depending on where the wall is, they'll hit it before we even get it finished." He handed the pictures back.

"What I was wondering was, is there a good paint you can use to cover this up?"

"You mean like, anti-graffiti paint? Sure, it's out there. But any kind of primer will cover it up. Sherwin-Williams makes a good one, works on masonry, wood, metal. PrepRite. They say it's graffiti resistant."

"Okay, thanks," Rigg said.

"Sure. Good luck getting the little punk. Or punks. We've seen a few of these kids hanging around the jobsite, waiting for us to leave so they can get that nice new wall. There's usually at least two of 'em, and those pictures you got look like a lot of work for one dude. Maybe you got at tag team."

"It could be. Our people think he's a lone wolf, though."

"Hmmm. Well, I'd rather you found Blunt and my van." He shook his head. "It ain't like Niko. He's a good worker. We never had any problems with him. But he got a call, Tuesday afternoon, and he was pretty shook up. When we were done, we all left the jobsite to come back here, but he never showed."

"How did he get a call?"

"On his cell phone. Everybody's got one from the company. Come to think of it, the son of a bitch stole that, too. I better cancel the service." The foreman turned to one of the clerical people in the office, getting ready to have her make the call.

"Wait a minute," Rigg said. "Before you do that, maybe we can do each other a favor."

"Shoot, boy," the foreman said. "I'll do just about anything for a police, drives a red Porsche and gonna get my van back. Need a wall put up? You want your car polished?"

"That won't be necessary," Rigg said. "But speaking of phones …"

Thursday morning

The late-morning sun beat down on Kalihi as Rigg walked back to the Porsche. The list of leads in the notebook was getting longer by the minute, but he felt the clock ticking down. Almost noon and more stops to make. The air conditioning in the Porsche wheezed a little cool air at him, but he suspected that was one of those not-so-little Porsche problems that was going to cost really big bucks to fix.

His companions kept up with him through the Kalihi traffic, Rigg making it easy for them, signaling his turns and stopping early for yellow lights. His destination was no secret;

he was heading back to the station to use the two tools invaluable for the modern investigator, his phone and the computer.

The Cave was quiet, and Rigg waved to the hidden camera before he sat down at the computer. He ran Stella again, looking for anything in her background that linked to what he now knew about Blunt, finding nothing. He did better with the license number of ZNT's van, which had received two parking tickets in the last two months for violations near Stella's Date Street apartment. Both had been issued in the early hours of Saturday mornings.

Tuisuga called from the prison to say that Stella Roddick's name had appeared on Blunt's approved visitors list. "She's the only person on there. No family, nobody. When she quit coming, he got no visits at all."

Rigg spent a half hour on the phone to Blunt's cellular provider, running numbers and asking for help with any calls that might have been made in the last day or so. He also checked all of Stella's phone bills against Blunt's, not surprised to see a lot of overlapping numbers. The two had obviously stayed in touch after Stella quit going to the prison, and it looked like Niko was driving over to see her on nights when he didn't have to be at work the next morning. He wondered if the van had been out on Sunday night or Monday morning, parked where it shouldn't be on Date Street.

Twenty-Three

Thursday afternoon

Ed Chin had seen the red Porsche in the parking stall on the lower level before. Assuming it was one of Narco's seized cars, he made a mental note to have it moved to storage. Parking was always at a premium in HPD's garage. This afternoon, though, he saw the parking sticker indicating that the car belonged to someone who worked in the building, and that pissed the Deputy Chief off. Porsches clearly weren't suitable vehicles for any sort of police service except for undercover work. No respectable officer should be driving any exotic, sports or luxury cars. No one could afford this car on a police officer's salary. It reflected poorly on the entire department.

So he'd worked himself into a fine snit by the time he got to the Porsche, intending to get the number off the parking decal. Chin had a Standard Operating Procedure for dealing with snit-causing irritants. He always started by finding out where the offender worked, and then he made life miserable for that person's boss, who should have had the supervisory skill and good judgment not to let the irritant get irritating in the first place. The supervisor would take the necessary action to correct the problem, and if he or she didn't, Chin could always go to that person's supervisor, repeating the process one level up.

Chin whipped a pen from his uniform pocket, extracting a small green notebook. This pad, known behind his back to his subordinates as "the Snit List," contained observations leading to previous tantrums and the names of the causes. He opened it to a fresh page, wrote "Porsche" and the number from the parking decal. Then he walked to the back of the car to record the license plate, where witnesses later said he went completely berserk.

The only people who saw what happened were two detectives from Narcotics/Vice who were taking some evidence to the property room, but they were certainly impressed. Of course, everyone else in the building heard about it in the next 15 minutes, the story collecting embellishments like an electromagnet in a filing factory as it passed from phone to phone. These distortions make any historical recreation of the facts difficult, but evidence, such as bits and pieces of the Snit List, found as far away as the elevators, and the fact that Mrs. Tanaka took sick leave for the rest of the afternoon, leads us to believe that this tantrum was monumental, possibly even volcanic.

By the time the tale reached the country stations in Waianae, Wahiawa and Kaneohe, Chin had almost totaled the car with his bare hands. And when Rigg heard about it, the only way he could tell they were talking about his Porsche was the license number that started the whole thing. Everybody got that part right. He'd finally received his personalized license plate the day before and installed it that very morning. It looked even better than he'd hoped, tucked under the Porsche's massive spoiler. "THANX ED," it read.

Thursday afternoon

The Porsche strained under him as he soared up the Likelike Highway toward Kaneohe. Trees pressed close to the sides of the road, flashing past as the car lifted him onto the long straight before the face of the mountain. He backed way off through the tunnel, letting the surveillance catch up with him, the car back on the leash but happy again.

Alton Jarrell had seen the Double-crosser. The reports for his interviews were in one of the boxes Martin had taken, and Rigg, who had never met Jarrell, knew nothing about him other than what was in the HPD computer system. He didn't have a driver's license, but his file said he was on probation, and Bear provided a current address. The drive across the mountains made a good excuse to let the Porsche run.

Once you're through the tunnel and past Kaneohe, Kamehameha Highway winds along the side of the bay, sometimes with blue water only a few feet from the roadway, at times with towering green cliffs looming above you on the other side. This is the wetter side of the island, and the foliage hunches over the road, the houses fewer and farther between. Driving on the winding road that follows the shoreline, you're in a part of Hawaii still locked 40 or 50 years in the past.

At the far side of the bay from Kaneohe, past the little island known as Chinaman's Hat just offshore, and across from the ruins of the oldest sugar mill on the island, a string of little bungalows sits between the highway and the ocean. Alton Jarrell's house was not much more than a large studio, one big room that neatly held everything left in Jarrell's life. That was the first thing Rigg noticed, how neat it all was. A tidy yard, edged with orchids and other tropical flowers, a rock garden with raked white sand. The second thing Rigg noticed was the metal crutches and the prosthetic devices, two steel tubes that clacked and clanked as Jarrell came to the screen door.

Nobody had ever told Rigg that Jarrell was disabled. He said so after the witness looked at his badge and heard what the unexpected call was about, Jarrell waving him inside to a dining table next to the open kitchen.

"If you don't mind my asking …" Rigg said.

"How did it happen?" Jarrell snorted. "Cops did it. How you like that?"

"Cops? Police did this?"

"Said it was an accident, but ..." Jarrell moved stiffly across the room, opening a sliding glass door, the legs clacking. "Not here. Was in California. On my way to a meet. Raining, just like the day when I saw Amber. Only this time I stopped when I saw the wreck. After Amber, I always stopped. I pull up behind the car, get out, was gonna ask how everybody was. This cop comes over the hill, going way too fast, cannot stop. I was standing right behind the other car, and wham." He shrugged. "Took 'em both off. Right here." He pointed to a spot halfway between his hips and knees. "Couple months after you folks caught the guy."

"Jesus," Rigg said. "Man, I'm sorry."

"Why? You never did nothing. And they give me medical for life and a million bucks. How else am I gonna buy this place?" He waved his hand at the sliding glass door leading to the lanai and the beach beyond. "Beachfront, got waves and everything. Best I could do for a million."

"How did you know Amber?"

"I used to live in the same building as her in Kailua. She parked right next to me, yellow BMW. One of those little convertibles? Not too many of those around. That's how I knew her car."

"Did you see her that day?"

Jarrell shook his head. "Nah. I never did. Just her car, jacked up, the dude putting the tire in the trunk and the white van. The van was parked in front of her car. She was probably in there, staying dry. Raining pretty hard."

"How good a look did you get at the man with the tire?"

"So-so. They showed me a picture before, asked me if he was the one I saw. That was like, a few months after the thing with Amber. I said I didn't think so. I looked at him pretty good, 'cause I was trying to get something going with her, you know? So I was kind of checking out the competition."

"It's been a while. If I showed you another picture, you think you could identify the guy now?"

"I doubt it, dude. A lot of stuff's happened since then."

"Give it a shot." Rigg produced his makeshift photo spread, five pictures of men who looked like Niko Blunt and the man, himself. Jarrell flipped through the pictures, taking his time, holding up each one. When he was finished, he went back to Blunt's picture, putting it on the top of the stack and handing it back to Rigg.

"Did you check me out before you came down here, man?" Jarrell asked.

"Yeah. I looked you up, why?"

"So, you know I got busted a couple of years ago, selling coke."

"Yeah, but that's got nothing to do with this. I'm not here about that."

Jarrell nodded. "Okay. But you probably know I also spent a little time in the joint. Not too long, just six months. At Halawa Medium." He stared out through the sliding glass door at the narrow strip of grass to the beach and the ocean beyond, an endless horizon in front of him and the prison cell behind.

"There was this guy in there, and I remember the first time I saw him in the module, I was thinking, man, that looks a lot like the dude I saw that night. And he was in for robbery, but he talked all the time about people he killed. Scary. I always wondered if maybe he killed Amber."

Jarrell looked up at Rigg. "I can't say for sure, and knowing the dude like I do, I don't know if I'd tell you even if I was sure. But that dude," he pointed to Blunt's picture, "looks a helluva lot like Niko Blunt. And Niko looks a lot like the guy I saw with Amber's car."

"You're right about it being Blunt," Rigg said.

"I'll tell you one thing I am sure about, though," Jarrell said.

"What's that?"

"That's a dangerous son of a bitch. He could've killed eight girls, and done it smiling. That's how he'd do you, too. Smiling."

"Thanks," Rigg said. "I'll watch myself." He got up and put the pictures in his shirt pocket. "You know, it's amazing what they can do these days, the technology that goes into these artificial limbs. People can do almost anything they could before they ... you know ..."

"Yeah? You hear about anything that lets me do what I used to, give me a call."

"What did you used to do?" Rigg said.

"I was a professional surfer."

THURSDAY AFTERNOON

After a short stop at the station, Rigg squealed the tires coming out of the parking garage, letting the followers know they needed to be up and about. Places to go and people to do. The afternoon shift change had just concluded, several officers going off duty turning to watch the Porsche accelerate down Young Street. He thought for a moment about losing the surveillance, then slowed to let them catch up. With a slew of unanswered questions, Rigg wanted to get a few answers. He didn't care if he had company for this ride.

The afternoon traffic had started to thicken, cars slowing as the rush hour got underway, the Porsche rumbling impatiently, needing open road. Ignoring the clogged freeway, Rigg launched himself up the side of the Punchbowl crater, taking the more scenic road that winds along the crater's slope. He dropped back down into Makiki, then joined the commuters going home into Manoa Valley.

For Rigg, who'd been raised in Manoa, every trip back to the valley was like going home. He loved the green mountain palisade rising on three sides, the classic old homes under big, spreading monkey pod trees, even the misting rain that passed over some part of the valley almost every day. The old Manoa, the one with horse pastures and small truck farms he remembered from elementary school, had gone, but the charm lingered like the memory of a soda from the Japanese store on East Manoa Road, shared with a friend on the curb outside 40 years before.

His destination today was an older home that perched on one of the valley's walls. University of Hawaii sociology professor Dave Nakamura lived a few doors down from Rigg's parents. When he returned to school for his master's degree and then the Ph.D., Doctor Nakamura had been one of his advisors. Although he had retired, he still served on the faculty committee that oversaw Rigg's research, his criminology background dovetailing perfectly with Rigg's field of study.

"Hello, Kimo," he said, motioning him inside. "How's your dissertation coming?"

"I'm getting there. I still have a couple of classes, and then the comprehensive exams, but I'll be able to work on the dissertation full-time after that."

"I'm looking forward to it. But what brings you here today?"

"I've been working on a case that might be connected to the serial killings from a few years ago, and I've got some questions about the profile we had."

"I hope you don't think the killer's still out there?"

"It's possible. The man I'm looking at was locked up right before the eighth murder. He couldn't have done that one or the first, but I'm not so sure about the ones in the middle."

"Hmmm. That would mean you had two killers, both using the same M.O."

"Right. How likely is that? I mean, we considered the possibility that we were dealing with more than one person, but everything made it seem like just one man was responsible."

"How likely is it that you had team killers? You'll be surprised. It's unusual, but I read somewhere that team killers were responsible for a fifth of all serial killings, so there may be fewer of them, but they're just as deadly."

Rigg described Stella Roddick's killing, the post-mortem mutilation and his suspicions about Blunt. "Everybody I've talked to who knew him in prison said he was the type who could kill and like it," he concluded.

"Liking it. Yes, that's what sets these people apart. The psychiatrists call it 'folie à deux.' It means 'the madness of two.' Of course, it can involve more than two, even many, but in this case, it's probably just two people. Both of them may have psychiatric issues, but alone they're not as dangerous. It's when their madness combines, when they synergize, feed off each other, they become a true terror."

"Folie à deux? And there are examples of that in serial killer cases?"

"Quite a few, actually. Many more than you would think. Or hope. The L.A. freeway killers, Bianchi and Buono. They're a good example. Henry Lee Lucas and Ottis Toole. Totally depraved. They killed female hitchhikers and prostitutes all over the country. They were probably very dangerous by themselves, but together they were monsters."

"Streck and Blunt. I wish I could find something that would put the two of them together. Right now, all I've got is Stella. She's the only direct link."

"How well known was it that the Roddick woman was your informant?"

"I don't know. We never publicized it. She never went on *Oprah* or anything, telling people she ratted out the Double-cross killer. But people talk, and she could have."

"You should consider another possibility, that somehow this Blunt character found out who had informed on Streck, the other half of his madness. When he got the chance to kill and have a perfect alibi, he confronted her. From what you've told me about the killings, I can imagine that would easily be enough to frighten someone to death."

"I thought of it. He would have had to string her along for a while, almost four years. Or they were still seeing each other. It's possible she accidentally let something slip recently, and that set him off. But I've been seeing Stella as a victim, and you know, this folie à deux thing makes me wonder if she could have been involved."

"Male-female team killers? Alton Coleman and Debra Brown. They killed children, old people, whoever they wanted. Brutal sex crimes. And those two in Southern California. He was depraved, but she was a full participant, and even did a couple of the killings on her own, and just as viciously."

"I had this theory, kind of thought about it before, but I wondered if he was sending us another message with the double crosses."

"What was that?"

"Well, he always made two X's. That's 2x in algebra, or times two. Some people thought he was saying, 'there's two of us.'"

"It's possible. The organized serial killers will do that, send little messages."

"Rigg shrugged. "It came up before. We thought of all kinds of possibilities. Somebody else said, 'what if he's saying criss-cross?' Maybe that meant we should be looking for somebody named Chris. Nobody knew anything for sure."

"Or maybe it was Roman numeral 20."

Rigg laughed once, a short bark with no humor in it. "That came up. Like maybe he was going for 20 victims. We were on about the fourth one at the time, so that idea cheered everybody up. I'm telling you, we thought of everything."

"Yes, well, I wouldn't worry too much about the messages, if any. They're not likely to help you now. What's important is the evidence you have that there were two killers, and at least one of them is still out there."

"What else should I be looking for with Blunt?"

"He's alone, now. From what you've said, there's nobody else in his life. That's likely to make him more unstable. He likes prison, maybe feels empowered there. He's not going to be restrained by a fear of going back. Has he got any other place to go?"

"I don't know. I haven't found any."

"Hmmm. Did you find Stella's clothing or jewelry? Her driver's license?"

"I don't think so. Her driver's license was in her purse at the apartment, but she was nude when she was dumped."

"He's keeping trophies, then. The same thing happened with the earlier killings, as I recall. So he has to have them somewhere."

"The van will be way too hot for him before very long," Rigg said.

"He must have someplace. Find it and you may find the evidence that would tie him into the earlier killings."

"I'm looking," Rigg said.

Thursday evening

On his way out to the car, his cell phone rang, Blunt's cellular provider calling to update the information on his bill. They said he'd gotten a call from a payphone in downtown Honolulu on Tuesday afternoon, and a few calls since. He hadn't made a single outgoing call after Tuesday, and they said the phone appeared to be turned off, which Rigg already knew, having called it a couple of times himself, getting the answering message. His hope that he could pinpoint Blunt's whereabouts or at least narrow them down by tracking the cell phone obviously wasn't going to work, but it had been a good try.

Rigg had an affidavit to write, but he knew it would never float unless he got more information, so he reluctantly turned the Porsche into the rush hour traffic and back to Kaneohe. This time he took the back roads behind Punchbowl, cruising down through Honolulu's oldest Chinese cemetery, hooking up with the Pali Highway in Nuuanu, motoring slowly as a curtain of rain descended on everyone on their evening commute. He passed the point near the reservoir where Amber Wheatley's yellow BMW had stopped, traffic moving faster toward the tunnels. Alton Jarrell's view of the two stopped cars and the stranger with the tire would have been no more than a snapshot. In the rain and the gathering darkness, an ID would be just about impossible.

Half an hour later, he pulled into the parking lot at Stella's former residence, the townhouses looking just like they had four years earlier. Rigg remembered where Stella parked, sliding the Porsche into the empty spot. He started with the next door neighbors, everyone home now after work. The Iwamuras on the right knew Stella well, but they hadn't heard about the murder. Rigg didn't enlighten them.

"Sure, she's here a lot. Haven't seen her for a few days, but she comes and goes," Mrs. Iwamura said. "I think she's got a boyfriend or something, because she's not here all the time. Her space is empty a lot of nights."

The resident manager said Stella and a couple of other tenants rented their places from a Japanese man who lived in

Tokyo, never came to Honolulu, and hadn't raised the rent since he bought the places. "They've got the sweetest deal in the place," the manager said. "Paying half of market value. I'm the only one in the complex who pays less, and my rent's covered by the association."

Joe Kam, in the townhouse across a narrow strip of grass and a board fence from Stella's, said he'd heard she was dead. "No cops been around, though. I thought you guys would be here before now."

Rigg said he was just tying up some loose ends, and had Kam ever seen anyone else there at the townhouse? He thought about it and finally said he hadn't. "Saw her on Sunday, though. Not this Sunday, she was already dead. The last one. She was here that night and during the day." Kam said he'd talked to her briefly, and that was the last time he'd seen her.

When he pulled out, the green Camry and a Mustang fell in behind, the little convoy hurrying back through the rain and the mountains toward home, Rigg carrying with him what he hoped was probable cause as the pain rose like smoke behind his eyes.

Twenty-Four

Friday morning

"SUCS, Detective Rigg."

There was a long pause while the caller contemplated the greeting. "What did you say?" the voice finally said.

Rigg checked the caller ID on his phone. Edmund Chin. "Oh, hi, Chief," he said. "I was just identifying myself and my unit, like the manual says."

"You said 'sucks.'"

"No, I said 'SUCS.' Special Unsolved Crimes Section. SUCS. And Detective Rigg. I said that, too. I thought about doing it the other way around. You know, 'Detective Rigg, SUCS.' But then, well, how would that sound? People might think I was saying 'Detective Rigg sucks.' They might wonder if I had a self-esteem problem or something. I think this way sounds a lot better."

Rigg thought Chin's breathing had gotten a little ragged, was going to ask if he'd talked to a doctor about getting more exercise, doing something about his blood pressure, but decided to let it go.

"I don't think so," Chin said coldly. "I don't think it sounds better either way. Change it."

"Okay. Well, thanks for calling, Chief." Rigg hung up, then sat back and waited for the phone to ring again. It took about a minute.

"You see us, Detective Rigg?" he asked when it did. The line hummed at him for a few seconds, Chin digesting the question and its implications.

"You see us?" Chin asked.

"No, I can't see you. I can hear you, though." Rigg said. "You sound fine. A little out of breath, maybe."

"What the …? You said 'You see us.'"

"No, I said I *can't* see you. I said I could *hear* you. That's how a telephone works. If we had one of those Internet phones with a camera, I could see you."

The line hummed, that same sound of ragged breathing again in the background.

"I can't hear you anymore, though," Rigg said. "Maybe you should talk a little louder, or I know, why don't you call back?"

"No, God damn it! I'm not going to call back!" Chin bellowed. Rigg winced. Poor Mrs. Tanaka would be getting an earful. He thought maybe he would send her some flowers. A get-well bouquet. Or maybe a box of manapua. He knew she liked the dumplings with their char siu pork fillings. But Chin wasn't finished. "I want to know why you're saying that," he said.

"It's the new greeting. The last time you called, which wasn't that long ago, you said to change it. You didn't like 'SUCS.' I think you said it sounded like SUCS sucks, so you wanted it changed," Rigg said.

"I know what I wanted." There was a pounding noise in the background. It sounded like Chin was beating on the new koa desk everyone was talking about. "What did you say?"

"I said, 'you see us.' Uniform, Charlie, Sierra. That's us, the Unsolved Crimes Section. You see, ass?"

But Chin was not falling for any more Laurel and Hardy routines this morning. With a noise Rigg happily imagined was either the Deputy Chief being strangled at his desk or several of his molars being ground down to the gums, Chin wrestled himself back into full control. "Never mind that," he said. "I need you to report to my office for instructions at four p.m. today. That's 16 hundred. Do you understand?"

"Four o'clock, your office. Got it," Rigg said. "Thanks again for calling. I'll work on the greeting." He hung up.

As the printer spit the pages of his affidavit out onto the desk, Rigg leaned back in the chair and examined the little holes in the ceiling tiles. Up to a point those had been two of the more entertaining phone calls of the week. He guessed that Chin's blood pressure might have set new fourth floor records. This was, however, a small comfort when taken with the sad fact that when the fun ended, Kimo Rigg would still be sitting in a basement room with nothing official to do but chase a teenaged graffiti artist and count the days until his retirement took effect.

And if that wasn't bad enough, he could also count down to the exact moment when he would walk into a room full of people who would be greeting him with handcuffs and his Miranda warnings. He had seven hours left until that moment arrived.

Friday morning

Rigg spent an hour of that time finishing the affidavit for a search warrant he'd prepared for Stella Roddick's old townhouse. Sandy had been slightly discouraging the night before. "You've got to be kidding me," she said on the phone, when he'd called to outline the probable cause he needed to get the warrant. "It sounds good, but I can't even begin to tell you how many problems there are with that, that … thing."

"Like what, for instance?" he said.

"Like the fact that your best information is four years old. *Four years*! The courts don't like it when it's four days old. You think you can get some judge to sign off on that? Not to mention the fact that no deputy from my office will look at it."

"I think I can find a judge," Rigg said. "And I already

talked to a deputy. She said, and I'm quoting, 'It sounds good.'"

Sandy laughed. "I see. It's an inside job. And I just figured out who you're going to take it to. Kevin Lee."

Now Rigg laughed. "Hey, I never thought of him. Thanks for reminding me."

"Right, you completely forgot about the District Court judge who also happens to be your high school classmate and your golfing buddy. Oh, please."

She agreed to meet him at Judge Lee's court in Pearl City the next morning, though, and he promised to work on his affidavit overnight to "at least clean it up a little." When he arrived at 9:30, Sandy was waiting outside the courtroom. He gave her the folder and they went inside and found a seat.

"Speeding violation, your honor. Driving 40 in a 25," Eddie Sylva, the courtroom deputy, read from his docket sheet as another in a long procession of traffic violators stepped forward. The end result of a well-publicized crackdown on what the newspapers had proclaimed "speed demons."

"Okay, how are you gonna plead, Mr ... is it Asuncion? Guilty or not guilty?" Judge Lee peered down at the defendant, a short Filipino man in worn work clothes. It might have been Rigg's vantage all the way at the back of the crowded courtroom, but he didn't think Mr. Asuncion looked especially demonic or even very speedy.

"Guilty, I guess. But I have explanation."

"Okay. Let's hear it."

"How much longer before Kevin's done, do you think?" Rigg whispered to Sandy, who was skimming over his affidavit.

"He'll break at a quarter to 10," she said, not looking up.

"Hmm. All right. 40 in a 25, that's pretty fast, Mr. Asuncion," the judge said, when the defendant finished. "I'm going to make it $50 and costs. See the bailiff there and don't speed any more. Next case."

Sylva reviewed his sheet and called the next defendant. The little courtroom was full, 15 or 20 people waiting for their chance to hop onto the rapidly moving judicial assembly line. Five solo bike officers, resplendent in polished leather and carrying their motorcycle helmets under their arms, stood near the door of the courtroom, opened to allow a breeze to circulate among the throng inside. Four attorneys chatted in low tones on the other side of the courtroom, waiting like Rigg for the break and the calling of the ten o'clock misdemeanor calendar.

"Okay, guilty then," the judge was saying in a bored tone. "45 in a 25, that's pretty fast, Mr. Maxwell. I'm gonna make it $75. See the bailiff, there. Next."

At this rate, Rigg thought, we'll be breaking early. His classmate was cranking out the cases, although it didn't sound like he was having much fun.

"50 in a 35, that's pretty fast. You've been here before. I know I've seen you. Let's say $150 and costs. And stop driving so fast." The judge shot back the sleeve of his robe, checking his watch as a low murmur ran through those remaining. "Next."

"Hundred and fifty bucks. You watch," Rigg said to Sandy. "It'll slow down now. Everybody's gonna want to plead not guilty or really explain themselves now that the money's getting serious."

"Hush. You'll get us thrown out." Sandy was on the last couple of pages of the document. She finished them quickly, looking up at him. "Is that it? Is that all you've got?" she whispered.

"You don't think that's enough?"

"It's still pretty thin, Kimo. Plus, it's still four years old."

"No statute of limitations on murder."

"That's not the point, and you know it. This is just so old, and her connection to the old crimes … well, it's hard to follow."

"You think Kevin's going to have a problem with signing it?"

"He's the friendliest judge you'll ever get. If he won't do it, nobody will. I wouldn't," she said. "The warrant would never hold up when it gets to court."

"Yeah, it will," Rigg said. "The townhouse is still rented in Stella's name. She's the only person living there, and at the moment, she's not living anywhere, 'cause she's dead. There's nobody else with standing to challenge the warrant. If I find anything, I wouldn't be able to use it against her, but I can't do that anyway. And Kevin will sign it."

"Well, then. After this is over …"

The crowd was thinning out as it got closer to 10. In front of the bench now, a kid who was literally holding his hat in his hands was launching into his preemptory justification for traveling twice the posted speed limit. "Okay, judge. I know it's pretty fuckin' fast. But I can explain," he started, as the crowd cracked up.

"I don't know, Kimo," Judge Lee said, a few minutes later in his chambers. "It's weak. I mean, when I first read it, I thought the date was a typo. Couldn't you have gotten this four years ago?"

"We didn't have any reason to suspect Stella back then. She was the informant, and we asked around and didn't find any connection to Streck. She looked clean."

"Well, you do establish that she was living at the Kaneohe address recently, that much is solid. What I don't get is why you'd think there would be evidence against Blunt there at her place."

"What I'm looking for is any evidence connecting Stella with Blunt, and to see if I can find someplace he might be staying. I found the picture in her other place, the apartment, and it's reasonable to think she's got other pictures, address books, papers or whatever that put her together with him."

"I'm going to sign it, but it's going to be litigated if you find anything. They'll lose, of course, since the only person with standing to challenge the search is dead, but I guess you knew that already."

"Yeah, thanks, Kev."

"Good luck. Eight murders. That's a lot more interesting than what I'm doing." He signed the affidavit and the search warrant, standing up. "Five more hours of traffic and DUI cases. It doesn't get any better than that."

"Nope," Rigg said. "But cheer up. We've got an 11:00 tee time at Pearl Country Club on Sunday. Hopefully I'll be telling you all about how I solved the big case while I whip your butt."

Rigg didn't say it, but he also hoped Judge Lee wouldn't be presiding over his arraignment on Monday morning, having to set bail for an old friend who'd missed their golf date.

TWENTY-FIVE

FRIDAY AFTERNOON

The townhouse looked just like it had four years earlier, only emptier, Stella having permanently departed. The parking space in front was also empty, and Rigg pulled in, getting out and waiting for one of the CIU cars to come into the lot. A white Mustang edged around the corner a minute or two later, Rigg waving at it when it started to back away. He walked over and leaned down to the driver's window, the two detectives looking flustered. He didn't know either of them.

"Hey, how you guys doing?" Rigg said. "Listen, I've got a search warrant for that unit right in front of my car, and I'm gonna execute it right now. Here's a copy, so you know I'm not burgling the place. I don't think there's anybody in there; the owner's dead. But if you hear any shooting, I'd appreciate it if you'd come in and help me out."

The detectives looked at each other, then at Rigg. "Ah, what the hell," the driver said. "You need some backup going in?"

"No, I think I'm okay. You folks just hang loose, I'll be out in a couple of hours. After this, I've got to go down to the main station. I'm supposed to see Chin at four."

"Yeah, we know," the driver said. "We're supposed to bring you in if don't show."

"No need. I'll make it. But if I'm still in there past 3:30, come in and get me."

The doorbell echoed in the townhouse, Rigg knocking loudly, announcing himself and his search warrant through the closed louvers next to the door. When nobody answered, he started trying keys from Stella's ring on the door. The third one turned in the lock, the door opening easily.

"Hello? Police officer. I've got a warrant." There was no response, but Rigg heard a scraping sound above him, and he drew his gun, covering the stairs to the second floor. He broke into a sweat despite the air conditioner's chill. "This is the police. Anybody up there, come down now. We've got a search warrant." Only silence came back down the carpeted stairs.

Keeping one eye on the staircase, Rigg cleared the rooms on the lower floor, satisfying himself that he was alone, at least in this part of the house. The place had a lived-in feel, full cupboards and dirty dishes in the sink, a Sunday *Advertiser* from the day before Stella died scattered in front of the TV. He thought maybe he'd found Stella's real home, and turned to the stairs to find out for sure.

He climbed slowly, the memory of the noise he'd heard earlier gripping, tugging at him, slowing every step. Halfway up, a gray and black cat whipped past his legs and down the stairs, diving into the kitchen. That could explain the noise, he thought. Or maybe it had come from the residents in the unit on the other side of the wall. Either way, his search of the second floor turned up no living creatures other than a few cockroaches in the bathroom, Rigg edging in and out of each room, his nerves settling with each one cleared. Standing in the hallway at the top of the stairs, he eased his gun back into the holster and took stock of his situation. He had exactly three hours before he needed to be in Chin's office, and he still wasn't sure what he hoped to find in Stella's townhouse. "It had better be something pretty damn spectacular," he said to the empty rooms.

Heading back downstairs, he dropped a copy of the warrant on the dining table, went to the door and waved to the Mustang, then started rummaging through the cabinets.

He found some cat food and put out a bowl for the animal, guessing it was probably starving if it had been locked up for over a week.

In the living room, he found papers in Stella's name, mail and bills, and some things for Blunt, too. A man's clothing and shoes were in one of the downstairs closets. Under the couch in front of the TV set, Rigg found a Smith and Wesson .357 Magnum. He thought about trying to preserve it for finger-prints, opening the cylinder gently, letting the six cartridges slide out, not touching them. He laid the empty revolver on the coffee table, feeling around under the couch and chairs for more surprises.

Video cassettes without labels were piled in a box under the TV. He pulled this out and set it aside, along with a photo album and a stack of old phone bills. The top sheet showed a number of collect calls from Halawa to Stella's home number. The connection between Stella and Blunt was getting stronger every minute.

Upstairs in the master bedroom a king-sized bed took up most of the space, and a dresser held some more male clothing mixed in with Stella's. A box full of loose photographs and more papers joined the pile of things on the bed he was planning to take downstairs. The other bedroom, obviously a spare, held quite a few male items, some with Blunt's name on them. It looked like Stella had been holding Blunt's things for him pending his release from prison. He was planning to do some weightlifting, by the looks of it; there was a set of free weights in the closet. That brought Rigg to the only part of the house he hadn't yet searched, the attic crawl space above. He went downstairs and got a bar stool from the kitchen counter, carrying it back and setting it under the access panel in the hallway outside the bedroom door.

Pushing the plywood panel up and into the crawl space, the noise echoing in the empty house, Rigg tested the flashlight once, then put his head and shoulders up through the hole into the waiting oven. Although a round louvered window grudgingly let in a little light and maybe some air from the parking lot outside, the temperature in the crawl space had spiked in the afternoon sun. It could easily be 120 or 130 degrees in here, Rigg thought, shining the light around, dismayed to see boxes stacked on plywood sheets stretched across the rafters in one corner. He'd hoped to find the space empty, and no need for the search that would require him to linger more than a few seconds in air almost too hot to breathe.

He wondered what Stella had kept up here, how any of it had kept from melting in the oppressive heat. He decided to take a quick look in each box, dropping it through the hole for a more thorough examination if the contents looked interesting. A stepladder lay across the beams, resting on top of a flat box that said it contained Christmas decorations. He levered himself up through the hole, the heat squeezing him. Crawling over the rafters, careful not to put any weight on the ceiling panels, he reached the stack of boxes, his shirt already soaked and sticking to him like a wetsuit in the darkness. Shifting a box, he cracked it open, shining the light inside. It was half full of clothing and papers, not carefully packed, but apparently thrown in haphazardly.

He reached for a familiar shape, pulling out a Hawaii driver's license, suddenly chilled to see Amber Wheatley's smile frozen forever in the DMV's flash. Her name, printed next to the picture, confirmed his identification, and almost in a state of shock, Rigg turned his flashlight on the other contents of the box. Pieces of jewelry, credit cards and a set of car keys on a chain with a plastic flower lay atop a pile of yellow cloth. He remembered that Amber's co-workers said she'd been wearing yellow the day she disappeared.

With the eerie sense that he was reaching back into Amber's grave, Rigg drew out the yellow dress, putting the light on the rust-colored stains at the neckline and shoulders. Her assailant hit her several times on the head with a metal object, possibly a tire iron, the medical examiner had said, something that would cause a lot of bleeding and could easily create this type of staining. Holding the dress out in front of him, the light playing on the yellow fabric, his eye caught a small reflection in the darkness beyond. He tilted the light in that direction, peering over the boxes at the shape in the shadows.

Niko Blunt, shirtless and thickly coated with sweat, crouched on one of the rafters, the light hitting him and shining off his tensed muscles. With an animal growl, Blunt lunged at Rigg, blowing straight through the boxes he'd been hiding behind and hitting Rigg chest high, knocking him backward, the flashlight spinning off into the darkness.

With Blunt's head under his chin and the momentum of the charge carrying them both, Rigg twisted as he fell, trying to land between the rafters, bracing himself for the impact. They crashed together through the ceiling, falling the six feet to a bed below. Rigg hit one side and bounced to the floor, while Blunt landed almost in the center, the mattress collapsing into its frame. As plaster and fiberboard rained down around them from the shattered ceiling, they both tried to adjust to the sudden change in their surroundings, Blunt squinting for a moment in the bright sunshine, but up quickly, coming at Rigg again, both arms swinging, his eyes now wide and wild. Rigg had barely straightened when Blunt hit him again, driving him through a pair of louvered closet doors, both men falling. Rigg again was on the bottom in a tangle of boxes and bedding, trying to get to his gun, Blunt pounding at him. The broken doors and the mess of clothes around them kept Blunt from landing any solid blows, but Rigg was pinned almost immobile. He tried kicking upward, getting a knee twice into Blunt's body as the closet shelf and clothes bar collapsed, burying both men in more of Stella's stuff. Rigg felt Blunt start to pull back, maybe hurt.

Shaking off the rubble from the closet, Blunt backed out, turning away and falling over the end of the bed, then scrambled toward the door as Rigg levered himself up to follow. Blunt staggered to his feet, heading for the top of the stairs, and Rigg tried to pull his gun while he freed himself from the jumble of debris, lurching to the door.

At the top step, Blunt hesitated, putting out a hand for the railing as Rigg hit him from behind, planting his shoulder in the middle of the big man's back and shoving, propelling him out over the stairs. Blunt hit about a third of the way down, tumbling to the bottom, and Rigg finally freed up his pistol, limping down the stairs, his right leg suddenly not working, something broken, maybe.

Incredibly, Blunt was up, moving shakily around the banister toward the living room, Rigg screaming at him to stop, remembering the Magnum on the coffee table, not wanting to kill the man, his leg giving, falling the last three steps to the downstairs landing. When he rose, he saw Blunt scooping up the Magnum, turning arm outstretched, the two of them facing off. Rigg was partly hidden by the thick newel post at the bottom of the stairs. He tucked himself tighter in behind the post and lined up his sights on the middle of Blunt's chest, streaked now with plaster dust and sweat. Blunt pulled the trigger, once, twice, three times, the hammer falling on an empty cylinder each time, the clicks echoing in the silence. They panted at each other for a minute, then two, the seconds ticking away, neither one looking away from the other's face, both thinking about escape as the third minute went by.

"There's nowhere to run," Rigg said when he got a full breath. "I'll shoot you or the ones outside will. Either way, you'll never get out of here alive. Put the gun down."

"Fuck that. You gonna shoot me?" Blunt said, his first words to Rigg. "I know how it works. I've seen people die. It takes awhile, most of 'em. I could still be able to get you." Blunt used his free hand to wipe the sweat out of his eyes.

"I don't want to shoot you. I want both of us to go out through that door and walk out of this place in one piece. Go someplace and take a shower."

"Don't give me that shit. You said you were gonna kill me and that's what you came here to do."

Surprised, Rigg almost lowered his gun, the words were so unexpected. "I never said I was gonna kill you. I came here to search the place. I didn't even know you were here."

"On the phone, motherfucker. You told me, you were gonna cut me up, just like you did Stella. Said you couldn't wait."

Now Rigg did lower his gun to stare at Blunt, the light through the vertical blinds on the lanai door striping the other man. He aimed again at Blunt's chest.

"What the hell? You think that was me on the phone? That call you got on Tuesday?"

"Yeah, it was you. How would you know about the call, if you didn't make it?"

"How about because your foreman told me you got all shook after somebody called you so I checked your freakin' phone bill?" Rigg said. "I don't know who made the call but it sure wasn't me."

Blunt thought this one over. "You don't really sound like him. The dude told me, said he didn't care where they put me, or where I tried to hide, he'd find me. He said Stella told him everything before she died. Said she was begging to tell him. And he knew stuff." Blunt hesitated, staring at the floor, lowering his gun. "He knew stuff only the two of us knew."

"About the killings," Rigg said.

"Yeah. She never would have told him unless she … unless he made her. He said everything she told him we did to the girls, he did to her. Did he?"

"I'll tell you everything I know. But first you've got to put down your gun. It's no good anyway, I emptied it. You're under arrest for escape."

Blunt shot a quick look around, spotting the cartridges lying on the table, calculating, not liking the odds, shoulders slumping, maybe surrendering. "What about the murders?" he said.

"You just admitted them to me. You're going to go down for them, too."

"What's the worst that can happen to me? Life in prison, right? Hawaii doesn't fry you."

"Life without parole," Rigg said. "This is Murder One. Multiple homicides. The only way out is if the governor commutes after 20 years."

"I'll go to fucking prison. That ain't no big deal. I just don't want this asshole cutting on me like he did Stella."

"That's not a problem. We can take care of that."

"I ain't talking about protective custody. P.C.'s for punks. Punk City, we call it. I ain't going there."

"Okay. We'll put you someplace else. Put your gun down." Rigg said.

"How do I know you'll put me somewhere this guy can't get at me?"

"We've got a special deal with the feds for that exact thing. If we need to, we'll put you in a federal joint on the mainland; you'll do your time there."

"Shit, I can do federal time easy. That's like ice cream, those places."

"All right. I'll personally work it out with the feds."

"What do I do? How does this work?"

"First you put the gun down on the floor and kick it over here. Then you put your hands on your head. Then you don't move an inch until I tell you to. That's how it works."

Blunt thought about it for what seemed like a long time, Rigg holding his breath until the man bent down, easing the Magnum to the floor. Straightening up, Blunt put both hands on top of his head, looking over for more instructions.

"Give it a push this way with your foot. That's good enough," Rigg said when the gun slid a few feet his way. "Now turn around, take a couple of steps toward the wall, stop and get down on the floor." Blunt hesitated, the wolf-like eyes back on Rigg's face, calculating.

"I could've taken you, you know," he said.

"Maybe. But that's over now. Turn around. Take two steps, and get down on the floor. Face down."

This time, Blunt did as he was told. Rigg waited until he was prone before retrieving the Magnum.

"Now, don't take this the wrong way," Rigg said. "But I've got to get those guys outside in here somehow, and this is the only way to do it. Turn your head this way so you know I'm not shooting you, but I've got to shoot something. Cover your ears."

Rigg pointed his gun up at the ceiling and cranked off three rounds, spacing them out, then turning the gun back on Blunt as the plaster dust settled around him like drifting snow. "That should fetch them," he said.

Moments later, a pounding came from the front door. "Rigg," a voice said. "You okay? We're coming in."

"I'm okay, don't shoot, but get in here."

The door banged open, the two men from the Mustang framed in the rectangle of light. "Jesus, man, what the hell's going on? Who is this guy?" one said, moving warily into the room.

"He's an escapee from Kalihi and he's got some stuff he wants to tell us. You got cuffs? Let's get them on him so we can talk."

More detectives came through the door, guns drawn, as the first two advanced on Blunt, bringing his arms back and cuffing both hands behind him. Rigg looked up at the three new holes in the ceiling, hoping for a moment that he hadn't damaged the graveyard in the attic where eight girls were buried. He sat heavily down at the dining table, his right leg screaming at him, watching the newcomers crowd the room. He recognized one of the detectives, John Correa, an old beat partner.

"Hey Johnny, you're in IA now, right?"

"Yeah."

"I guess I have to report an officer-involved shooting," he pointed at the ceiling. "I'm gonna be writing reports about this for a month," he said.

FRIDAY AFTERNOON

Rigg's cell phone was gone, lost somewhere between the attic and the ground floor. He borrowed one from one of the CIU detectives, calling Hata, asking for people from Homicide and the Crime Scene Unit, giving the address and a few details. He checked his watch: he had an hour before he had to leave.

"Tell 'em to send an ambulance, too," one of the CIU people said. "You're bleeding like hell. Your back's a mess, and this one's cut up, too."

"I'll be okay. You guys got a first aid kit in the car? Bring it in. And if you've got a recorder, bring that, too." His back felt like it had been scourged, but Rigg was pleased to note that the headache that had been his constant companion for days had completely vanished.

With Correa and a cassette recorder, Rigg took Blunt to the dining table, sending everybody else outside to wait for the CSU. Turning the recorder on, Rigg advised Blunt of his Miranda rights, asking for and getting a clear acknowledgement that he understood and waived them. Blunt wanted to talk, and he blamed it all on Stella.

By the time the first car from Homicide screeched into the parking lot, they had the outline of the whole story, Correa shaking his head in amazement after Rigg said they were taking a break. "We just cleared eight murders."

"Nine, actually. Don't forget, he said Stella killed Streck," Rigg said.

"Jeez. I'll tell you one thing, that's one cold mother."

"No shit. He's actually looking forward to going back into the joint."

Cal Kamaka came through the door, looking for Rigg, heading straight for him when Rigg stepped back from the sink. "Damn, Kimo. You look like you went through a meat grinder."

"I'm turning this over to you, now. I've got to get back to town for my meeting with Chin at four. You need to put a couple of people on Blunt, finish the interview, get all the details from him. Maybe Johnny can stay with you; he knows what ground we've covered already. Unless you've got to go with me," he said to Correa.

The IA detective shrugged. "No problem. I'll square it with the boss later."

"Okay," Rigg said. "He's admitted to doing six of the Double-cross murders and says Stella did all of them. He says it all started with a scheme she cooked up to get rid of Carol

Collins, and then it sounds like it just got out of hand."

"Is he telling the truth?"

"There's a bunch of boxes up in the attic. Send the CSU people up there first. I only got to look in one of them before he jumped me, but there were trophies in there, just like the profilers said there would be. Amber Wheatley's driver's license, her credit cards and the dress she was wearing when they snatched her. Blunt says you'll find things from all the other girls up there."

"They kept the stuff all this time?"

"Yeah. And check this out. He says Stella couldn't wait until he got out so they could start up again. He said she had all kinds of plans. First thing she was going to do when he got paroled was go buy a van."

"God. Do you think he killed her, too?"

Rigg glanced back over at the dining table, where Blunt sat, head down. As he watched, the big man's head sank to the table, his energy, like Rigg's, all drained away. "No. There's something else going on there. I don't think he's gonna be much help on that."

Except for the mess he and Blunt had made, the second floor and the attic were still virgin territory, Rigg said. None of the CIU or IA people had gone upstairs, so the evidence technicians and Homicide detectives could work it like a regular crime scene. "Tell 'em to be careful in the attic," Rigg said. "It's hell up there, and that's not just an expression. I don't know how that son of bitch stayed alive in there for as long as he did, waiting for me to go away, all that heat."

"It's 3:30, you'd better get going," Kamaka said. "You're gonna need to change your shirt."

Rigg stood in the front door, taking in the scene one more time, knowing he wouldn't be back. All this would be someone else's problem, now. The last of the adrenaline that had pumped into his system during those moments of terror upstairs finally leaked away, leaving him empty and depressed. He turned and walked through the cluster of CIU people standing in front of his car. "Let's go get this over with."

FRIDAY AFTERNOON, 4:00 P.M.

The crowd in the foyer outside the Deputy Chief's office fell silent when Rigg limped in, staring at him. Rigg recognized a lieutenant and another detective from IA, and there was Jerome Martin, looking pleased, and Rick Hata, wearing a frown. Ed Chin couldn't contain his own grin, relishing his big moment.

"Wow," Rigg said. "I had no idea this was such a big deal. We putting a task force together? Kind of late, though, now that I already cleared it, don't you think?"

Chin waved everyone into his office. "No, sergeant, we already have a task force, and it's managed to solve a more important crime than the one you've been working on."

"Really?" Rigg said. "I wouldn't have thought there was anything bigger than nine homicides. Seems to me it was pretty important before."

"What are you talking about?" Chin said.

"The serial killer. The Double-cross case. I thought that's what we were all here for."

"Stop changing the subject. That case was already solved. And you're not supposed to be working on it, anyway."

"Yeah, I thought it was solved, too, until a couple of days ago. Then I found out the guy we thought was good for it, Ray Streck, who, by the way, was conveniently dead, didn't do it. In fact, the real Double-crossers killed him, too, so he's actually victim number nine."

Confusion reigned for a minute or so "while Chin tried to get his railroad back on track," as Rigg put it later to Silafau.

"You should've seen them. He couldn't figure out what the hell was going on."

"We haven't got time for ancient history," Chin said. "These men are going to question you about your involvement in a homicide on Monday morning, and your gross insubordination and failure to follow direct orders."

"That would be the Roddick thing. I haven't got that one solved yet," Rigg said. "This has been a busy week for me. I cleared nine murders and a bank robbery. But I'm working on it."

"You're not working on anything, anymore," Chin screamed. "You're finished. Finished!" He gestured to the IA Lieutenant. "Get him out of here."

"Wait a minute," Hata said, who already knew quite a bit more than he was letting on. "What's this about the Double-crosser?"

"It's Double-crossers, plural," Rigg said. "I've got one of them over in Kaneohe talking to Homicide. He confessed, gave me the whole story. I'd still be talking to him, getting all the details, but I was ordered to come up here at four for this thing."

"This is some kind of trick," Chin said, glaring around the room, Martin and the IA people confused, Hata examining his fingernails, leaving the floor to Rigg.

"Trick? No, I'm not that clever," Rigg said. "I don't do tricks. I'm just trying to solve an unsolved crime, like you told me to. And right now, I think Major Hata and Marty and I should all go back over to the Windward side and finish interviewing this crumb before he decides to lawyer up and tell us to get stuffed. I've got nine down and one to go, and to be honest with you, I'd kind of like to go 10 for 10 if I can."

"No. You're not going anywhere, except down to the cellblock. As a prisoner," Chin said. The Internal Affairs lieutenant looked appalled.

"Chief, you said we were treating this as an administrative matter. You can't threaten to arrest him. We won't be able to use any statements he makes." The lieutenant said this under his breath, as though nobody else in the room could hear.

"I'll save you the trouble. I'm not making any statements," Rigg said. "Administrative or otherwise. If you want to arrest me, go ahead. But you'd better have the goods, because Mike Stone's waiting for me to call and let him know what's happening."

Hata's cell phone rang. "That's probably Kamaka, now," he said. He listened for a minute, snapping the phone shut, looking at Chin, who made one of those "hurry up" motions with his hand, wanting to get his train back on schedule.

"It's like Kimo says. Blunt's repeated his confession to Kamaka, on video this time, and the CSU people say they've got evidence from all eight of the Double-cross killings. They say they found photos of five of the girls, bound and naked. Blunt's in some of them, and he identified the evidence and said he and Roddick did the killings. There may be something in writing, too, like a journal Stella kept." Hata faced Rigg. "It looks like you were right. Good job."

"Good job?" Chin said, gagging on the words. "I'll decide if it's a good job or not. Who said they could search this place? Who authorized the warrant?" he demanded.

"That would be Judge Lee," Rigg said. "He signed the paper this morning. I ran it by the prosecutor's office last night. And it sounds to me like it paid off like a Vegas slot machine."

"It sounds to you? You're not supposed to be doing anything on this murder. You're assigned to a graffiti case. You just admitted to a clear violation of a direct order. I'm instructing Internal Affairs to open an investigation of insubordination and conduct unbecoming. You're to comply with their requests, and you're required to answer their questions."

"I know the rules. I've been there before, remember? You can order me to answer, but anything I say can only be used in an administrative proceeding. But you just threatened to arrest me, which makes it criminal, so I have a right to a lawyer and I don't have to make any statements."

Chin looked to the IA lieutenant, wanting a little support, not getting it from that quarter. The silence in the room stretched, everyone calculating their next move. Finally, Jerome Martin put up his hand, almost like a school kid. Everyone turned to him. "I got a question," he said. "If Blunt didn't do it, then who killed Roddick?"

"Damned if I know," Rigg said. "And that's your case, Marty. The DC told me I'm finished on that one, so you're gonna have to figure it out on your own. Me? I've got a tagger to catch. And if I can't go back over to Kaneohe, I'm going out on sick leave for the rest of the day. My leg's killing me." He turned to walk out, the others sucking in their breath as they saw Rigg's back for the first time. The shirt was torn and soaked with blood from his adventures in Stella's townhouse. "Yeah, and my back isn't feeling too good, either," he said.

Twenty-Six

"Wait up, Kimo." Hata came down the hall to the elevator where Rigg stood. "Let me take you over to the ER, we can talk on the way."

"Thanks, Rick. I'm not really in any condition to drive."

The elevator doors opened and they got in, Hata pushing the button for the basement. "So, are you in a condition to talk?"

Rigg laughed. "I'll make it. My leg feels like it's broken. I must've hit something. I fell down a couple of times."

"What's up with your back?"

"I fell out of the attic … through the ceiling. It's a good thing there was a bed there."

"Jeez. What happened out there?"

"I should start at the beginning." The doors opened and they walked to Hata's car, a big Buick. Rigg waited while Hata got a towel for him to sit on, then slid gratefully into the passenger seat. "Man, I'll tell you. I love that Porsche, but it's a beast to drive. All that shifting and crap in Honolulu traffic. You're working all the time. You might have the right idea here, got the quiet comfort thing going. Hey, you ever hear somebody say they'd rather be lucky than good?"

"Yeah, so?"

"I've been going along the whole week thinking Blunt killed Roddick, been focused on that like a damn laser beam. Just like Marty and those guys were focused on me for the same thing. But I got lucky, and they didn't."

"I don't get it."

"I didn't either. I kept coming back to Streck, and the fact that he was dead. We knew for sure that he was the Double-crosser, believed it with all our hearts, you know? Everything pointed to the guy, even the DNA evidence.

"But here's the thing, what if the killer didn't work alone? There's precedent for that. You remember those two guys in LA, the Hillside Stranglers. That one up in Canada and his girlfriend. The D.C. Sniper, Muhammad and that kid, Malvo. The two in Phoenix killing homeless people. But the ones I got to thinking about are Tom Whitman and Steve Norton. They got convicted in California for torture killings of teenage girls. Driving around in a van, picking girls up off the street. They tape recorded at least one of the murders. We got a copy of the tape when we were doing our investigation. I couldn't sleep right for weeks."

"I thought the task force looked at that angle. The two-man deal."

"We did. But only for a minute, because the profilers said it was one man, and the Amber Wheatley witness only saw one man, and when Stella put us onto Streck, he's a loner. When Streck died, the killings stopped. Nobody wanted to think there might have been two of those monsters out there."

"Like you said, the evidence against him was solid."

"Yeah. Too solid, it turns out. But I'll get to that. Anyway, I start off with Stella. She's dead, and somebody's obviously made it look like a Double-cross killing, right down to the crosses cut into her feet. And if Streck's dead, who else knew about that part of the M.O.? Just the people on our side. But we're not killers, so what's the real killer saying? He's saying, 'the Double-crosser is still here.' But who is he?

"When I got the picture, Stella and Streck and Carol Collins in the bar, I decide maybe Carol's boyfriend and Streck are tighter than we knew. Maybe he's the other half of the tag team. You know, the shrinks have a term for that, 'folie à deux.' That's something else I learned this week. Folie à deux. It means 'the madness of two.' They feed off each other, push each other. Alone, they might not be capable of pulling it off, but together, watch out."

"That would explain Blunt's alibi. He's covered for two, but his partner could have done those and they did everybody else together," Hata said.

"Right. The first one and the last one. They're the different ones. We couldn't see that back then, we were too busy focusing on how they all looked alike. What they had in common. But the first and the last were different after all."

"The last one is Stella."

"No," Rigg said. "She's a victim, but not of the Double-crosser. He's freaked about whoever killed her, knows whoever it is has him lined up next. That's why the son of a bitch was living there in her place for three days. Hiding out with the lights off, not making any noise. The only thing he did was watch the TV news to see if we'd caught Stella's killer."

"So, he didn't do that one? You're sure about that?"

"Yeah. He was convinced I came to kill him. He said the killer called him on Tuesday, told him you're next. I checked with his cellular company; he got a call from a payphone downtown Tuesday afternoon. So, when I show up, he just flipped out, ran to the little secret hideout he and Stella had kept. Only he screwed up. If he'd just sat on the trap door, I'd never have gotten the damn thing open. I would've just given up, never would've gone into the attic."

"And she kept stuff from the killing up there."

"Yeah, she'd kept the townhouse when she went on probation, but never gave that address to her P.O. She had a really sweet deal with the owner of the townhouse, some Japanese guy in Tokyo. When Blunt got out, they were going to get married and move back in. They had to be married, because they're both on probation, can't see each other, otherwise. And he said she couldn't wait to start killing again, talked about it all the time."

"She was the leader? Not Blunt?" Hata said.

"That's what he says. I kind of believe him. He's a bad boy, but I think he's actually a little scared of her. He says she cooked up the scheme. It started out as a way to get rid of Carol Collins. Stella wanted her gone so she could have Niko, and he wanted her gone because she was making noises about child support and paternity for the kid."

"How was Streck involved, then?

"This is all hearsay, because Niko was locked up, but he says Stella just framed him for it. She went out with him a couple times, like that party where the picture was taken, and then she borrowed his van, told him she needed to move some things, kind of came on to him a little. Once she had the van, she gets Carol to go with her, killed her, cut her up, including the double crosses on her feet."

"Why on her feet?"

"She just wanted something distinctive, 'cause she knew she was gonna do it again with some stranger. Originally it was just going to be one more, to lock in the alibi for Niko. She figured we'd decide one guy killed both girls, and Niko, who was somebody we'd automatically suspect for killing Carol, if he had a solid alibi for the first one, he'd be clear on the second one. Which is just exactly what happened."

"But they didn't stop with the second one."

"Nope. Blunt says she liked it, told me she liked to play director. 'Do this to her, do that to her. Make her scream.' And he got into it, too, because he's really a vicious son of a bitch."

Hata pulled the Buick into the emergency room parking area at Queen's Hospital, throwing the blue light onto the dashboard, and both of them got out. Rigg's back had stiffened, and he took a few seconds to straighten before walking toward the ER door.

"Anyhow, Stella's really the key part of the team. Remember how we wondered why the girls would get into a van with Streck? Well, Stella had this blue Jeep, fun-looking car, and she's a female alone, the girls never saw it coming. She'd get them in the Jeep, feed 'em some story, then drive to where Niko was waiting. He had a van, too. A red one Stella had bought and never changed the title. The girls just felt comfortable around another girl, and before they knew it, they were in the van. We should've seen it."

They signed in at the ER desk, Rigg taking a chair in the corner, Hata sitting next to him. "Maybe," Hata said. "20-20 hindsight, though."

Rigg sighed and looked up at the ceiling. "I know, but we owed those girls 20-20 foresight, and they paid for it. You remember Karen Scott? UH student, lived in Waikiki. Goes out for a jog. Stella's out jogging ahead of her, pretends to fall. Scott stops to see if she's okay, and bam, Blunt's on her, getting her into the van. Bye-bye.

"They had it set up like one of those tiger traps in India, where they set out the goat, shoot the tiger when he shows up. Stella was the goat, only Niko was the tiger. That's how she did Streck, too. Called him up one day after Niko went back into the joint, said let's be friends again, goes over, gives him an O.D., then plants the stuff in the van and the house, runs off and makes her phone calls. It was a pretty good scam, and only a couple of really sick bastards could have pulled it off."

The nurse called Rigg's name and he stood.

"I'll be here when you get out," Hata said. "I'm going to go outside and call Cal and see if there's any news. Thanks for filling me in."

Rigg stood for a moment, shaking his head. "I can't get over the fact this whole thing started because somebody wanted somebody else's boyfriend. And he didn't want to pay child support. Ten people dead. Makes you wonder where God is, doesn't it?"

TWENTY-SEVEN

THEY STARTED ON THE BEACH that afternoon, Rigg still recovering from the fall. His ankle was sprained but not broken, his back healing. Two hours of hard paddling had the muscles burning, but Bear was ready for more. "I'm still game. Let's take the two-man for a run, go out to the buoy," he said. Rigg stood on the beach and squinted at the sun, already dropping low on the horizon. "I don't know, man. You think we've got enough time before sunset?"

Bear stood up. "Hell, yeah. And if not, it ain't gonna be the first time we came back in the dark."

Two-man outrigger canoes look more like ocean kayaks, low to the water, sharply pointed at both ends. Made of space-age composites, they're lightweight, strong and built for speed. You don't sit in a modern two-man canoe, you sit on it, and with Rigg in the forward seat, Bear stroked hard in the back, propelling the two-man toward the channel marker and the surf beyond. Turning the canoe upwind, Bear kept the boat just outside the breakers, in the calmer waters where the big swells rose up and rolled away under them in long, greasy mounds. Rigg set an easy pace, giving himself some breathing room after the open ocean workout. Ahead and to his left, a big set of waves rolled into the surf spots known to local surfers as Tongg's and Rice Bowls.

"It's breaking at No Mans," he said over his shoulder to Bear, naming an offshore break. "Don't let us get caught inside on the way back."

"No sweat. So, you done with your big case? The one you were calling us on?" Bear said.

"Which big case? The tagger or the serial killer?" Rigg said.

Bear laughed. "I'm glad you solved it."

"Technically, I haven't solved either one. I think I'm close on both, though. You know, here all along, I've been telling people about coincidences," Rigg said. "But I missed the biggest one of all."

"Yeah? What's that?"

"Well, I mean think about it. I work the Double-cross case, and out of the clear blue, bam, a new murder with almost the exact same M.O. turns up on my doorstep. Literally. That's a helluva coincidence, the killer dropping her off four years later, practically in my lap."

"Yeah, I see what you mean."

"Right, and let's say that it isn't really a coincidence, say that the killer knew I lived there, and he dropped her off so I could find her, so I could make the connection."

"It's possible," Bear said.

"I know it is. And it makes sense, if what he's trying to do is get me looking at the old cases, maybe re-focus on somebody other than the man we all know is dead."

"Let's pick it up to 72 a minute, take it out past the buoy," Bear said. The canoe leapt forward, hissing through the water, bearing east against the swells, hard upwind work ahead.

They worked together in silence, the two of them moving in unison, hammering it out for long minutes, the canoe gliding steadily in that eerily smooth but cherished perfection that only happens when paddlers, boat and ocean are in complete harmony. Bear steered the canoe farther offshore, the tempo changing as the swells built, the tradewinds that rushed down Diamond Head's slopes knocking the tops off the waves in foaming whitecaps.

Now the sea fought them, Rigg keeping the pace up,

his arms and shoulders and especially his damaged back screaming at him. The canoe rode up the swells, lunging down the far sides, spray kicking up around them. Minutes went by, paddles flashing in the waning sunlight, one stroke for every beat of a normal heart, and then they were at the buoy. Bear turned the canoe for the downwind leg, the two of them resting for a moment as the swells passed beneath them, paddles across their legs, the Diamond Head light shining brightly for a moment, revolving away, then flaring again.

"You can almost see my house from here," Rigg said. "If you know where to look. And that's what got me thinking. How many people knew I'd moved into Stone's cottage? It was a short list. Then all I had to do was try and figure out the connection to the Double-cross case."

"Did you get it?" Bear back-watered with his paddle, turning the canoe's bow downwind, the sunset now in front of them.

"Not right away. I kept coming back to the message. That was the Double-crosser's big deal; everybody he dumped was a message. He was telling us, 'It's me again. I've got the power and you can't stop me.' Only what's he saying with Stella? Stella's different from all the others. She's older, she's not damaged the same way the others were, not mutilated at all. But she's right there, saying, 'Look at me.' So, I went back and looked at her and the others. You know how we link murders together? How we figure out there's a serial killer out there?"

"No. How?"

"We look for similarities. If the murders are enough alike, odds are the same guy did it. But this time I went back and looked for differences. What made one victim different from the others? It wasn't obvious, but I found it. Found her, really."

"Who was it?"

Rigg took in the sunset, the golden ball almost touching the horizon. "Oh, I don't know, Bear," Rigg said finally. "Why don't you tell me?"

"Let's go. Take it easy. Enough to catch the swell. We've got to get back, now. I guess you mean Carol Collins."

Rigg dug in his paddle, setting an easier pace. "That's her. Once I got that part figured out, once I knew Carol was different from the other victims, everything else started falling into place. It took a big guy to get Stella out of the condo. Somebody strong enough to carry a 135-pound woman and a surfboard over his shoulder. Somebody who had a connection to Roddick. Somebody who she'd open her door for. And the clincher was, it had to be somebody who knew where I lived. Like I said, there weren't too many people like that. Mike Stone, Nate, Iwa, Sandy. And you."

Bear was silent for a moment, matching Rigg stroke for stroke, but not saying anything as the boat slid over the water. Finally, he spoke. "C.C. was my daughter. Her mom and I never got married, but I helped her out till she died. When Laurie got the cancer, I couldn't take care of either of them. We gave her hanai to Laurie's auntie. When Laurie died, C.C. just stayed there. I kept away, let Moaniala raise her, but I always thought of her as mine. We were an ohana, still."

"How did you figure out about Roddick and Blunt?"

"It started with the picture. I found it in C.C.'s things. She had a bunch of pictures of her and Niko. They were going together for a while, made the baby, had some rough times. But she had that one picture of her and Streck and Stella. I knew who he was; his picture was in the paper after he died. And when Stella came to us on probation, I recognized her. I talked to her about the case and she told me the same thing she told you. She never saw Streck except in the parking lot, never knew anything about him. But I had the picture, so I knew she was lying."

"And you'd have talked to Carol's auntie, so you knew Stella was going after Carol's boyfriend. Made the connection."

"Yeah. I knew he couldn't have killed Carol, but she had a reason. And I talked with her a few times. She was cold inside, I could feel it."

"So, she knew you already. That's why she let you in that night."

"She's got to open the door. It's part of her probation. 'Subject to surprise inspections.' I put the picture there in the apartment. I thought you'd be involved in the case and you'd recognize Streck or C.C., you'd make the connection. If you didn't right away, I would have called you."

"You should've called me. Told me what you knew before all this."

"And how would you prove it? I couldn't do it. Not without a confession from her or Niko. God, I hated her so much. They just robbed C.C. of her life. Took it from her casual, like they were picking up a penny off the street. Over a bum who never loved her and a few hundred dollars a month in child support. I'd have given it to them. So, they robbed the baby of her mom. I knew what that was like; I lost my own mom when I was little. So, I scared her, made her think I was going to do her like they did all the others. All I was gonna do was get her to confess, then let you go after both of them. But she just, like, all of a sudden died. I wasn't sorry, though, I was glad she was gone, especially after she told me about the other girls and what she and Niko did. I figure I did the world a favor."

"Why didn't you kill them?"

"I was going to. I thought about it. But I was kidding myself. Believe it or not, I'm not the killer type, and after Stella,

I couldn't. Enough people died already. I drove around, trying to figure out what to do, then I thought, I'll leave her by your place. If she'd lived I was gonna just drop her off back at her apartment. I mean, who's she gonna tell? When I couldn't do that, I thought I could get you to go after him for me, so I dropped her by your house. She told me enough about the other girls so I knew how to lay her out, knew about the way they cut them. I thought you'd see it and you'd go after him."

Rigg slowed, not in any hurry now to get home and face the pain waiting on shore. "Well, it worked," he said. "I went after him. God damn it, Bear."

The sun had set out past Barber's Point, the western sky ahead a carnival of reds and golds, shining clouds piled almost to heaven. Behind them, darkness chased down the ocean swells that pushed them toward the lights of Waikiki and Honolulu beyond. The boat picked up one of those swells, a big one, already piling up and cresting, the canoe leaping down the face, the ama dancing on the water.

"Stay on this one, we can ride it all the way to the beach," Rigg said, shipping his paddle, letting the steersman do his job.

Bear played the wave, moving the canoe higher and lower on the face, staying in the power, the spray, tinted with the sunset's colors, flying past them, the wind singing in their ears. Rigg closed his eyes, shutting out the vision of what had to happen when the ride ended, opening them when he felt the boat's attitude change, startled to see how close to shore they'd gotten. Caught inside at No Mans.

"Bring her head up, she'll go in," he shouted.

The canoe, turned now almost perpendicular to the face of the wave, dove toward the bottom. "Aloha no, brother," he heard Bear say, before the boat's nose disappeared into the black water at the bottom of the trough. The full power of the swell consumed the canoe, flipping it, driving it down, stopping it short, then, as the wave passed, covering everything with the quilt of white foam that lay over tons of moving water. Diving clear, Rigg stroked downward to avoid the iaku and the ama, the wounds on his back shrieking at the contact with the salt water. He surfaced 10 yards from the inverted canoe, shaking his head to clear his eyes, and caught sight of a drifting paddle, catching it and heading for the boat.

He righted her easily, hopping back aboard and straddling it, expecting to see Bear swimming his way. The canoe rode high over another swell, the face starting to steepen as it piled up into the surf zone, but the water around him was empty. He called out without receiving a response, beginning to doubt, and tried standing on the canoe, falling into the water. A hundred or more yards out to sea, he thought he saw a splash, paddling to it, finding only spume from a passing whitecap.

After 20 minutes of paddling in a circle, he realized the current and the wind had pushed him at least a quarter of a mile, the Natatorium barely visible in the growing darkness. Reluctantly, he turned the canoe toward shore. The Coast Guard would be out all night, and he'd be on the beach in the morning when the sun came up, but he knew that the sea had taken his friend, and the Bear was no more.

TWENTY-EIGHT

SUNDAY MORNING, 2:00 A.M.

OZ-MAN 1, who was not 15, but 22 and easily old enough to know better, crept through the undergrowth at the base of the little hill, his objective shining brightly in the moonlight on the slope above him. The wall surrounded a private estate, most of it hidden by foliage, but one section, visible to the street below, lay open and inviting.

Twelve hours earlier, the wall had been painted, all of his careful artistry of a month before obscured by a thick coat of luscious tan paint. The art now covered had been one of his finest efforts, a riot of bright colors and wild shapes, a hidden message and his very overt statement of power over the wall and the man who owned it. An OZ-MAN 1 masterpiece, but all gone, now, and the master's heart sang, for some kind soul had provided him with a new canvas.

At the base of the wall he shrugged out of the backpack that held the tools of his hobby. He was dressed for a fast getaway, running shoes and shorts, and a t-shirt about the same color as the wall. If he had to run, he could be a block away in seconds, and then look like an ordinary jogger, out really late for some exercise. OZ-MAN 1 planned his operations like a NASA mission commander. He'd never been seriously challenged.

On the road below, a car swept past, the edges of its headlights just swiping the smooth, even surface. He stood for a moment, shaking the can and picturing his new creation when it was finished, shining bright and fresh in tomorrow's sunlight for all of Honolulu to wonder at. It was going to be beautiful. He made a long vertical stroke in black, the paint hissing in the silence, getting to about waist level when the light snapped on, pinning his shadow to the wall.

The first rounds hit OZ-MAN 1 right between the shoulder blades, the shock throwing him off balance and into the wall, his paint can falling away as the shooter walked the long burst down OZ-MAN 1's body. The pain was incredible, the tagger writhing under dozens of impacts, twisting in the relentless beam of the flashlight, turning to run, jackknifing in agony as the stream of punches centered in on his groin and legs.

The seemingly endless rattle shut off abruptly and OZ-MAN 1 heard something thump to the ground next to him. Whatever it was exploded with a pop, showering him with liquid that completely covered his face and arms and splattered the wall behind him with patches of bright color, mostly red and green.

Preoccupied with his own pain, OZ-MAN 1 did not see the man dressed all in black rise out of a clump of bushes just down the slope. He carried a paintball marker and wore a black mask with a plastic faceplate, and he walked to the tagger, snapping the flashlight off when he reached the wall, setting the marker to one side.

The man in the paintball mask held the writhing and sticky OZ-MAN 1 to the ground with one gloved hand, patting the tagger's shorts pockets with the other. He found the car keys first, then the wallet, jerking it out, flicking it open and extracting the driver's license. Hands in his crotch, OZ-MAN 1 cried into the fallen leaves at the base of the wall. He heard the man speak.

"Rang your chimes, huh? I'll bet that hurts like hell. But I know who you are, now, Dexter. And I can tell you, if I see any more OZ-MAN 1 tags up, anywhere, I'm gonna come find you and you're gonna wish I was using paintballs." The man turned and flung Dexter's car keys into the underbrush, then flipped the driver's license over the wall.

"You're gonna be black and blue for a few days, and pretty red for a few more; that's the stuff they use in bank robbery dye packs. It doesn't wash off. You probably don't want to go into any banks for a while either; they might get the wrong idea, but when you feel better, there's a can of paint and a roller there. I'm coming by here in the morning and that wall had better look just like it did when you walked up here. This ain't OZ-MAN 1's wall any more. This is Dexter's wall, now. Anybody else tags it, you get up here and fix it. You understand?"

Dexter groaned something that might have been a "yes" and rolled into a fetal position, clutching his flaming testicles. His forehead head bumped the gallon can of paint, and with crossed eyes he read the label. Sherwin Williams PrepRite primer in creamy tan. When he rolled back again, he was all alone. Gentle tradewinds rocked the branches above him, casting dancing moon shadows on the wall. Dexter lay there for a long time, thinking maybe he'd find a new hobby. Stamp collecting sounded safe.

In his car on Diamond Head Road, Ian Rigg passed the spot where Stella Roddick's body had been found, musing on the sad fact that some crimes just aren't meant to be solved. Sometimes you don't know the answers, and sometimes you know the answers but you can't do a damn thing with them.

"It sucks, but what can you do?" he said, as he turned into his driveway.

THE END

ABOUT THE AUTHOR

JOHN MADINGER grew up in Honolulu and spent most of his 30-year law enforcement career in Hawaii. As a criminal investigator with the U.S. Treasury Department, he has written textbooks on money laundering and confidential informants and has lectured around the world on financial crimes and criminal investigation. *Death on Diamond Head* is his first novel.